FUJINO OMORI

ILLUSTRATION BY
SUZUHITO YASUDA

Is it WRONG to TRY to PiCK UP GIRLS iN A DUNGEON?

VOLUME 13

FUJINO OMORI

ILLUSTRATION BY **SUZUHITO YASUDA**

New York

IS IT WRONG TO TRY TO PICK UP GIRLS IN A DUNGEON?, Volume 13
FUJINO OMORI

Translation by Winifred Bird
Cover art by Suzuhito Yasuda

Original Japanese edition published in 2018 by SB Creative Corp.
This English edition is published by arrangement with SB Creative Corp., Tokyo, in care of Tuttle-Mori Agency, Inc., Tokyo.

Yen On
1290 Avenue of the Americas
New York, NY 10104

Visit us at yenpress.com
facebook.com/yenpress
twitter.com/yenpress
yenpress.tumblr.com
instagram.com/yenpress

First Yen On Edition: March 2019

Yen On is an imprint of Yen Press, LLC.
The Yen On name and logo are trademarks of Yen Press, LLC.

The publisher is not responsible for websites (or their content) that are not owned by the publisher.

Library of Congress Cataloging-in-Publication Data
Names: Ōmori, Fujino, author. | Yasuda, Suzuhito, illustrator.
Title: Is it wrong to try to pick up girls in a dungeon? / Fujino Omori ; illustrated by Suzuhito Yasuda.
Other titles: Danjon ni deai o motomeru nowa machigatte iru darōka. English.
Description: New York : Yen ON, 2015– | Series: Is it wrong to try to pick up girls in a dungeon? ; 13
Identifiers: LCCN 2015029144 | ISBN 9780316339155 (v. 1 : pbk.) | ISBN 9780316340144 (v. 2 : pbk.) | ISBN 9780316340151 (v. 3 : pbk.) | ISBN 9780316340168 (v. 4 : pbk.) | ISBN 9780316314794 (v. 5 : pbk.) | ISBN 9780316394161 (v. 6 : pbk.) | ISBN 9780316394178 (v. 7 : pbk.) | ISBN 9780316394185 (v. 8 : pbk.) | ISBN 9780316562645 (v. 9 : pbk.) | ISBN 9780316442459 (v. 10 : pbk.) | ISBN 9780316442473 (v. 11 : pbk.) | ISBN 9781975354787 (v. 12 : pbk.) | ISBN 9781975328191 (v. 13 : pbk.)
Subjects: CYAC: Fantasy. | BISAC: FICTION / Fantasy / General. | FICTION / Science Fiction / Adventure.
Classification: LCC PZ7.1.O54 Du 2015 | DDC [Fic]—dc23
LC record available at http://lccn.loc.gov/2015029144

ISBNs: 978-1-9753-2819-1 (paperback)
978-1-9753-3077-4 (ebook)

1 3 5 7 9 10 8 6 4 2

LSC-C

Printed in the United States of America

VOLUME 13

FUJINO OMORI

ILLUSTRATION BY SUZUHITO YASUDA

PROLOGUE YOU'LL BE BACK

You'll be back.

Someone told me that.

"It's no good; I can't find Lyu anywhere," the human waitress Runoa said, shaking her head.

She had just returned to The Benevolent Mistress, the bar on East Main Street. It was shortly before opening time, and her words caused a sudden uproar among the other employees.

"Where could that girl have gone, meow? I'm sure she's playing hooky. Unforgivable, meow..." the catgirl Ahnya complained, flinging herself onto the table. Her words, however, had no bite to them.

"But this is the first time she's gone off without saying a word, leaving only a letter behind," Runoa said, gripping the piece of paper and sighing as if she was quite upset.

Lyu had vanished from the bar.

Without permission and unexpectedly.

She had left a note in her room in the back building, announcing in her beautiful penmanship that she would be away for a while and apologizing.

"She's disappeared now and then in the past, but...this time..."

Something felt different.

The staff of The Benevolent Mistress had sensed it and had split up a little earlier to search for their elven coworker in her usual haunts.

"She's been really tense lately, you know? So tense that whenever I saw her...I felt uneasy."

"Hey, you blackhearted cat, watch your mouth!"

"Whoops!"

Chloe covered her face with a hand in response to Runoa's

reprimand. The catgirl had been narrowing her eyes and looking completely unlike herself, but when she moved her hand away from her mouth, it was wearing its usual smile, as if she'd switched personalities once again.

"Meow...I'm just worried something happened to her, given she's someone who has been forced to do work dirtier than cleaning the sewers, meow. Or rather, that she made something happen, meow," she pronounced, swishing her cat's tail and smiling inanely.

Her worry was more premonition than insight—the premonition of one who knew about the past of the elf called Gale Wind.

"Hey now," Runoa said, scolding the catgirl's half-joking words for a second time.

She glanced at the corner where a girl with blue-gray hair sat wordlessly.

Syr remained silent, an expression of intense thought on her face.

As if to dispel the tension in the room, the two temporarily quiet catgirls began to chat noisily again.

"While the white-haired one is holed up in the Dungeon, Syr is down in the dumps, meow! I'm sure it's all one of his plots, meow!"

"Definitely! It's all the boy's fault, meow! To make up for it, I'll force him to let me bury my face in that ass of his, meow!"

"You two are disgusting! What in the world are you talking about?" Runoa said.

But even the ordinary scene of Ahnya and Chloe running their mouths and being scolded by Runoa didn't bring a smile back to Syr's face. That was because the serious elf, who always reproached the others so calmly, was missing from their circle.

Suddenly, the door to the room opened with a *bang*.

"What the hell are you idiots doing? Stop gossiping and get to work!"

It was the dwarf owner of The Benevolent Mistress, Mia.

Ahnya, Chloe, and Runoa jumped at their boss's shout and scurried out of the bar like so many baby spiders.

Alone now, Syr and Mia exchanged looks in the suddenly quiet tavern.

"Mama Mia...Do you know something?"

"If you don't know anything, how am I supposed to?" Mia replied curtly.

Syr was Lyu's closest friend.

The dwarf turned and left the bar.

"That elf is a real handful," she muttered on her way out.

"Lyu..."

Syr's whisper disappeared into the hushed bar.

Are you okay?

I remember that warmth.

I remember the hand the girl with the blue-gray hair extended to me.

I remember the smile of the girl who brought me back to the world of light after I had wreaked my vengeance, driven by raging emotions and a misplaced sense of justice, long after I had lost my reason to live.

She saved me.

Those women rescued me—those catgirls who worked at the bar and its crazy dwarf owner.

I feel as if that noisy, pleasant bar washed my body clean.

My body defiled by blood and filth.

My sky-blue eyes that had been burned to ash by the flames of revenge.

If someone was to ask me now what the most precious thing in my life was, I'd probably say The Benevolent Mistress.

That's how sacred everyday life with those women is to me.

All the same, my wounds never went away.

The emptiness from losing my familia, which was as important to me as that bar.

The palpable loneliness that would throb painfully at any chance.

Although I closed my eyes to them, I knew the black embers were still smoldering in my heart.

I would dream about it.

The shrieks that filled the air.

The horrible, piercing screams.

The tears stained red.

The violent last moments of those girls, once so beautiful and noble, kept rising before my closed eyes.

On mornings after I had the dream, I fought to overcome the writhing of my terrible emotions and the unbearable sense of loss.

My raging emotions were crying out.

It almost seemed like I could hear the lingering regrets of companions, their cries searing my body.

I would hold myself and dig my fingernails into the flesh of my arms.

In the shadow of the gentle light that The Benevolent Mistress shone on me, a small darkness lurked. For the past five years, I have been bearing two emotions in my heart.

So I may have known.

I may have known full well that if the chance presented itself, the dam would break and I would transform into an unstoppable monster.

There exists a certain dim underground maze.

Cold drafts fill its passages.

In that maze, there is a cesspool of Evil that the sun never reaches.

What I saw there made my hair stand on end.

"L-L-Leon!"

A voice of despair.

My name, drenched in fear.

The men shivered as they looked at me.

Time stretched out, and when the moment broke, the monster in my heart shattered its chains and roared.

"Leon?!"

I heard them call my name again.

It may have been the last thread holding me back.

But I shook off the voices of my comrades and surrendered myself to my raging emotions.

As the men ran in a panic away from me, I pursued them.

Wherever they run, whatever tangled corner of the maze they try to hide in, my desire will never stop screaming out within me until I pounce.

The flames from the black embers are spreading.

All too easily, they have transformed into hellfire.

You'll be back, Gale Wind.

My heart told me that.

And it was right.

As long as I do not overcome my past—

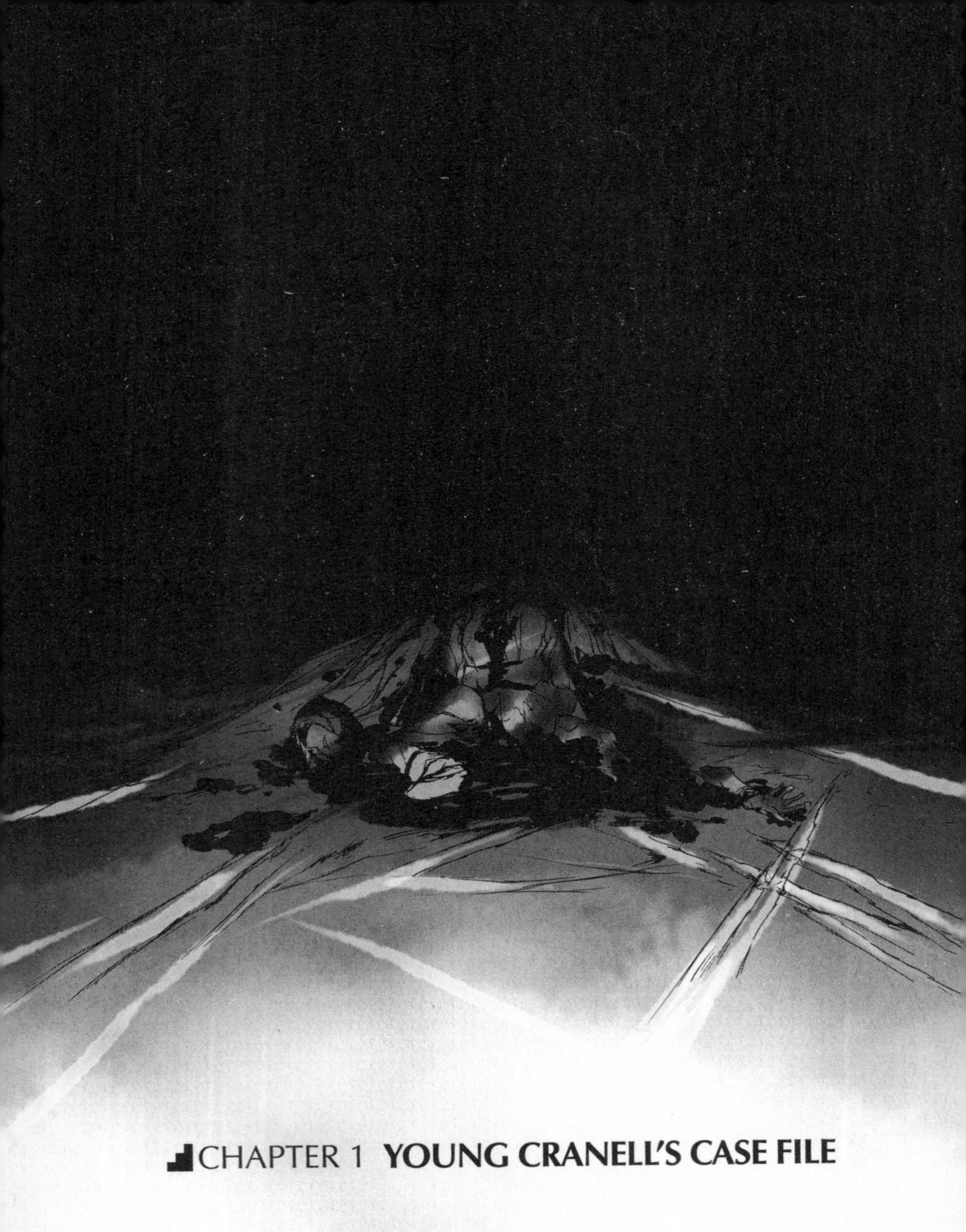

CHAPTER 1 YOUNG CRANELL'S CASE FILE

"It's awful..."

The adventurers grimace in unison the moment they see the scene.

Reddish-black stains are splattered everywhere.

In the center, sprawled like a doll, is a corpse.

It's the body of a fellow adventurer, pitifully shredded—or rather punctured—by countless stab wounds.

I have no words as I stand rooted to the ground before this scene.

"No way..."

It's Welf who spoke. He and the rest of my party have belatedly joined the group of adventurers who gathered after hearing about the incident. He draws his brows together as he lets out a groan.

Our current location is the eighteenth floor of the Dungeon.

We've returned to this safety point to seek treatment for the wounded members of our joint party—born from a faction alliance between *Hestia Familia* and several others—after we finally managed to overcome the Irregular moss huge we encountered in the lower levels, where we'd headed for our expedition. Right now, we should be planning a celebration to commemorate our safe return alongside *Modi Familia* and *Magni Familia*, who we met along the way.

That plan, however, has gone out the window with the appearance of this dead body.

"Oh yeah...it's definitely a murder. This is the work of a human not a monster..."

Bors, the head of Rivira, clicks his tongue as he stares down at the corpse. He and the noisy group of adventurers are gathered at the foot of an enormous island that rises from the marshlands on the outskirts of the town.

He's right. The wounds on the body are far too clean to have been inflicted by a monster's fangs or claws. This could have been done only by an adventurer's blade. Most likely, the lethal blow was what left a bloodstained hole in the adventurer's neck.

The entire corpse is covered in cuts that speak to the ferocity of the attack. There are wounds from a blunt weapon, too, including crushed bones and broken limbs. The bloodshot eyes are wide open…as if the adventurer had come face-to-face with something terrifying but was unable to do anything to fend it off.

"Ugh…" Haruhime groans, pressing a hand to her mouth.

"Please don't look, Lady Haruhime," Mikoto says, wrapping her arms around her friend's shoulders and blocking the horrible sight from her view.

Caught up in the wall of spectators, Lilly and Aisha exchange grim glances. Nearby, Ouka is standing tight-lipped while Daphne frowns. But the healer Cassandra is paler than anyone.

"Hey, Bell, are you okay?" Welf asks, sounding worried.

"…"

I can't find the words to answer him. I'm just staring in a daze at the adventurer's corpse.

My heart is beating uncontrollably.

Of course I'm shaken. Being at the site of another adventurer's death—at the scene of a murder—is a huge shock to body and soul.

But just as powerful is the feeling of dread that dampens my cheeks with clammy sweat.

"It was Gale Wind! She was here! She did this…!"

My breath catches at those words.

Yes, indeed, the name causing all this uproar among the adventurers is none other than Gale Wind.

"I saw it! I saw a hooded elf stab Jan like a crazy person and then run off!" screams the male werewolf, a resident of Rivira and the first to discover the corpse.

As he speaks the name of his deceased acquaintance, he hugs the body, drawing the gazes of Bors and the gathered adventurers.

"I've seen Gale Wind once before, with a bunch of *Astrea Familia* members. Those guys were as strong as monsters. Her face was hidden the whole time…but the sky-blue eyes I saw deep inside the mask were the same eyes I saw today!"

Perhaps because he is reliving the experience, the werewolf adventurer is shaking from head to toe as he speaks.

There's no doubt about it—the description matches hers.

But I still can't believe it.

I don't want to believe it.

How could Gale Wind—how could Lyu—do something like this?

"I'm sure of it! Gale Wind killed Jan!" the werewolf shouts.

Just as I'm about to shoot back, "Wait a minute now!" another adventurer speaks up.

"Now that you mention it…I saw someone in a mantle running across the fields."

"Oh, me too! They went straight to the Central Tree…and down onto the floors below!"

I lose my chance to interject as the witnesses speak up one after the next. It seems that multiple adventurers saw someone who looked like Gale Wind from various vantage points in Rivira, which is carved into a cliff and has excellent views of the surrounding terrain. Lilly, Welf, Mikoto, and Haruhime—all who know about Lyu's background—are stone-faced.

For some reason, Aisha is silent, too.

"…But didn't Lady Leon of the Gale Wind die five years ago? And even if she's still alive, why would she be causing trouble now?" Mikoto asks. She's among those who were won over by Lyu's struggle, and she's made up her mind to express her doubts.

"…I've heard rumors that the Guild and *Loki Familia* are planning a large-scale operation in the near future. Word on the street is that they discovered the secret hideout of the Evils' Remnants," Bors says in an uncharacteristically serious tone.

The words *secret hideout* give me an idea.

Knossos, the man-made dungeon.

The violent hunters who captured Wiene and the other Xenos were using that awful place as a base camp. It's a real incubator of Evil.

There is definitely some connection between the Evil that grew rank in Orario five years ago and Lyu, who was a member of *Astrea Familia*. I heard it from the elf herself on this very same eighteenth floor.

"If Gale Wind is alive and taking advantage of this new campaign by the Guild to become active again…this could all make sense."

"…!"

"Gale Wind is a crazy adventurer, driven by hatred for those who killed her familia members to crush anyone suspicious without giving them a chance to argue back. She'll kill anyone she deems to fall in the gray area…including merchants and Guild members," Bors continues, crossing his arms and gazing around at the crowd.

"Plenty of residents of this town know all about Evil. Actually, everyone here is a shady character. We're here in this Rogue Town because we couldn't make it on the surface with the Guild's crackdowns, and we had no other choice."

I've heard about the underground markets that exist here in Rivira, beyond the Guild's oversight, engaging in rampant illegal trading with adventurers. There are rumors that it's possible to buy illegal goods and even rare items like Status Thief, which is made from the ichor of deities. It goes without saying that it's all a gray so dark it's almost black.

Setting aside adventurers like us who stop here on our way to take on various floors, the people who live in this town are all involved in risky business. Bors's words must have hit home, because almost everyone standing around me shudders.

"Gale Wind may have decided that all of us, including Jan lying over there on the ground, fall on the black side," Bors says.

"Th-this isn't a joke, Bors! Sure, we've done more shady things in our day than we can count, but are you gonna stand for murder on the basis of suspicion alone?" the animal-person proprietor of an inn shouts.

"Yeah, we may be bad, but we're not connected to the Evils' Remnants!" an Amazonian merchant yells in a voice so shrill it's practically a scream.

That brings all the other residents of Rivira to start shouting as well.

In an instant, the level of excitement and the anger toward Gale Wind have ballooned.

"Bors, let's get her!"

I can't believe what I just heard.

"Jan, our fellow townsman, has been killed for something that makes no sense at all! Even if we live in Rogue Town, can't we at least fulfill our duty to the community and avenge his death?!"

Perhaps out of anger over the death of his acquaintance, the werewolf who first discovered the body is arguing furiously, his face bright red. As the heat of his argument spreads to the people around him, Bors crosses his burly arms and responds in a troubled voice.

"What you say is true...but I put my own life first. What happens to other adventurers is no concern of mine. You think I'm going to go after a Level Four monster like Gale Wind, who's blacklisted and on the run?"

"Speaking of her being on the run, isn't there a bounty on her head? The money some of the merchant associations put up should still be up for grabs, right?"

"Now that you mention it, I think the bounty was...eighty million valis?"

"—Listen up, everyone. I'm putting together a group to take her down!"

On hearing this, Bors waves his hands energetically.

"We will avenge our fellow townsman! We won't let anyone else take her head! The bounty money is ours!!" he shouts.

"Yeaaaaaaaaaaaaaaaaah!"

Bors has clearly become engrossed by his selfish desire. All he can see in his eyes is money. I can only frown. His words worry me. Welf and Mikoto seem to feel the same way. Each of the adventurers gathered makes his or her own selfish calculations, many shouting passionately.

All the evidence points to Gale Wind.

It's a shame, but that's the truth.

Another reason I feel so confused is because what Bors said reminded me of something.

It was something Lyu said to me once.

I let my emotions take over, and I wrought my vengeance.

It wasn't even justice.

If Lyu felt she'd discovered the Evil she couldn't forgive, and her cruel desire for revenge had returned…that may well have been motive enough.

Lyu, could you really have done this?

The image of a single elf standing before a mountain of corpses covered in fresh blood rises in my memory.

Her eyes carry a sense of brutality, as if she has been consumed by a cruel storm of dark emotions.

I quickly brush away the disturbing vision.

"Wait a minute!"

This time, I speak the words out loud, making everyone turn toward me.

There's no way Lyu would do something like this.

At the very least, I, who have heard her story, have to voice my doubts!

I still remember her expression, so full of pain and emptiness.

"Isn't it too soon to assume this is the work of Gale Wind?"

"What, are you accusing me of lying?!" the werewolf adventurer snaps back.

Something else is bothering me.

I confront him head-on.

"How did you know it was Gale Wind?"

"I already told you! I've seen Gale Wind before! She and the criminal who killed Jan are one and the same!"

"How long have you been living here in Rivira?"

The werewolf, who has been spouting off angrily, looks at me dubiously in response to my odd question.

"Huh? I've been here for years! You may not have noticed, but we've crossed paths in town quite a few times, Mr. Super Rookie!"

"So you were here four months ago when *that* incident occurred?"

"What of it?"

Yes, something is bothering me. And with the werewolf's response to my last question, the vague doubt turns to certainty.

Something here is off.

Properly speaking, it was three and a half months ago that the Black Goliath showed up. Lyu fought with us against it, right alongside the townsfolk of Rivira. This werewolf has just said quite clearly that he was here when that incident occurred. It doesn't make sense that he didn't notice Lyu at that time.

Of course it would be impossible to remember all the adventurers who were involved, since fierce battles were taking place all throughout the floor. But Lyu was right there alongside Asfi, holding back the floor boss the whole time. What's more, she used her powerful magic to fight it. There's no way he wouldn't remember that.

Given the situation, it's possible that no one wanted to turn her over to the authorities at that time. But Lyu's past didn't come to light after the incident, either. Judging by how Bors and the others are acting now, none of them realizes that Gale Wind was the adventurer who fought alongside them on the eighteenth floor.

But if her disguise was actually that perfect...could it be possible that the werewolf didn't know it was her when she was fighting so prominently during that incident, yet he recognized her here despite working with such limited information?

If possible, I don't want to doubt him.

I don't want to, but...

This guy is lying...!

I stare back at the werewolf, who's threatening me with his fierce gaze.

He doesn't know Gale Wind.

Something akin to an adventurer's intuition whispers the thought to me.

"...Rabbit Foot, are you saying the criminal isn't Gale Wind?" Bors asks.

Many of the adventurers encircling me have suspicion in their eyes.

Perhaps it's because the residents of Rivira trust the werewolf that they feel skeptical of my claim. That goes for Bors as well.

They're weighing the fugitive Gale Wind against the words of their fellow townsman.

It's clear who they trust more. No one is going to back me up when I defend the blacklisted elf.

If you want to say something, go ahead and say it. That's what the eyes surrounding me on all sides seem to be saying.

I almost back down, but I hold my ground.

Lyu wouldn't do this. That's what I believe.

"Gale Wind—"

I'm about to say that she's not the criminal when Aisha reaches a hand out and pulls me back.

"Stop."

"What?!"

"Sorry to put a damper on things. Now, what were you all saying?"

Aisha has stepped forward as if to take my place, and with her arms crossed beneath her breasts, she prods the crowd to continue.

Bors and the other guys are ogling her ample bosom and deep cleavage as she stands there with a bewitching smile on her plush lips. Bors starts in surprise after noticing the disgusted looks and clicking tongues of the women in the crowd, and then, after a deliberate cough, he continues the conversation as if nothing has happened. It's like he's forgotten I exist.

Aisha, who's totally used to confronting rough characters, silently jerks her chin as if to say, *Let's get out of here*, but I can't resist pressing her to tell me why she stopped me.

Just when I'm about to, though, someone pulls my right shoulder back.

"Calm down, Bell."

"Welf..."

Now he's arguing with me, too.

I close my mouth and nod softly as he looks down from a head's length above me with that big-brother look.

Our whole party steps away from where Bors and the others are talking about the hunt for Gale Wind.

"What do you think you're doing, leader?" Aisha asks as soon as we're far enough away. "It's not a wise idea to stand up for that girl."

"Lilly agrees. Given what's happened, we need to avoid making enemies here."

"But Miss Aisha, Lilly—"

"Who knows, people could even start suspecting that we're connected to the crime," Lilly continues.

"!"

Lilly's words jolt me.

I was so caught up in thinking about Lyu that I hadn't even considered that possibility.

...Aisha is right. I've failed them as a leader.

Even if I wanted to stand up for Lyu, I should have reacted more coolly. I was on the verge of dragging Welf and the others into something risky.

I feel deeply ashamed of my immature conduct.

"Damn, right when I thought you'd grown up a little, you go and act like a kid again," Aisha says.

"Sorry..." I say, looking at the ground and hanging my head.

Aisha laughs.

"It's not such a bad thing if you stay like that deep down."

"Huh?"

"You get all worked up for someone who's not even a part of your familia...Isn't that what other people like about you? I'm the total opposite, of course."

I'm surprised to hear her say that.

When I look around, I see Haruhime and Mikoto breaking into smiles while Ouka closes his eyes and grins, Daphne hunches her shoulders, and Cassandra looks down shyly.

Lilly and Welf are smiling broadly, too.

"Plus, if that straitlaced elf was here, I bet I know what she'd say."

Aisha turns up her lips in a totally unconvincing impression of Lyu.

"She'd say, *Mr. Cranell, that's a virtue of yours.*"

The light has gone out in the mum-shaped clusters of crystal on the ceiling of the eighteenth floor, and the sunset-less evening of the Dungeon has fallen.

We've returned to central Rivira and are gathered in the room where we're staying. The place we picked is Willy's Inn, a cheap hotel built into a cave. For the price, it's one of Rivira's nicer spots, and the room we're in now can easily accommodate ten or more guests. We've met up with Chigusa, who's been resting to recover from the parasitic vines that were planted in her by the enhanced moss huge.

"Based on the evidence, Gale Wind is the prime suspect... Unfortunately, that fact can't be changed," Lilly says, turning to the rest of us as we stand surrounded by bare rock walls and magic-stone lamps.

"But just like Mr. Bell said, a few points are troubling. Putting aside Miss Lyu's motives for the moment...While Mr. Bell was arguing with the others, Miss Daphne and I snuck a closer look at the corpse."

"Now that you mention it, I noticed you two were up to something..." Welf says, a bit surprised.

"To be honest, I didn't really want to." Daphne sighs reluctantly.

I had noticed that Lilly mysteriously disappeared when Aisha interrupted my argument. It seems they'd quickly decided on a plan among themselves.

Lilly says it was a big help that I was diverting the crowd's attention... but as I stand next to this cunning trio, I can't help feeling that I'll never live up to the true brains of the party.

"There were stab marks all over the body...But among those random blade wounds, there were also sharp wounds running down the arms and legs. I hate to call them clean...but they seem to have been inflicted with incredible speed."

"In other words..."

"It's extremely likely that those specific wounds were inflicted by Gale Wind. I just got a quick glimpse from a distance, but they looked almost identical to the ones from her shortswords that I saw before."

A tense expression spreads over Mikoto's face as Lilly speaks. Aisha continues the explanation.

"Most likely, she severed the tendons on his four limbs so he couldn't escape."

"Wh-why would she do something like that...?" Haruhime asks, her fox's tail quivering at the shocking image.

"What I'm about to say is pure speculation...but I'll bet she questioned the adventurer," Aisha answers.

Welf and Ouka, who have been listening to the conversation, gasp in surprise.

"No way! You mean the elf just extracted some information from the guy?"

"And once she got it, she left...before going down to the lower levels, as the witnesses said?"

"Well, there's plenty of reason to think she killed him after she made him talk," Daphne answers, as if that would be a totally normal thing to do. "But...isn't there something *fishy* about the act of stabbing him all over so blatantly, as if to put Gale Wind's anger and hatred on display?"

In other words, it could be a setup.

Someone else might have come across the adventurer Lyu left behind after her interrogation, killed him, and then stabbed him all over to cast suspicion on Lyu.

That's Daphne's unspoken implication.

"W-wow, Daphne...You're just like a detective!" Cassandra says excitedly.

"Shut up," she snaps back, trying to hide her embarrassment.

"Ergh!" the rebuffed Cassandra squeals.

Aisha continues her explanation.

"The townsfolk in Rivira are after Gale Wind's head. They're going to send out a hunting party for sure."

"That's terrible..." Chigusa murmurs, speaking for us all.

For a moment, silence takes hold of the room.

"If we want to clear Miss Lyu of suspicion...the most important thing right now is to get to her before they do," Lilly says, wrapping up the discussion.

We have to reach her faster than anyone else and find out what really happened. That's the first step.

Lilly looks straight at me with her chestnut-brown eyes as she explains what we need to do.

"..."

Everyone else's gazes gravitate naturally toward me as well. For a moment, I concentrate all my energy into my tightening fist.

What information did Lyu extract from the dead adventurer, and why did she head to the Dungeon? What in the world did she learn?

If someone else is the real criminal, why did they want to pin the blame on Gale Wind?

There's so much we don't understand.

But if she's involved in this incident...then my answer has already been decided.

"Let's go find Miss Lyu."

If she's been swept up in some sort of scheme, I want to help her.

Lilly, Welf, Mikoto, Haruhime, Ouka, and Chigusa all nod in agreement. It's time for us to repay our debt to the masked elf who has helped us countless times. From the mortal fight with the Goliath floor boss to the War Game and even during the battle in Daedalus Street against the Xenos, she has proven herself an invaluable ally time and time again.

Seeing that the boat has already left shore, Daphne and Cassandra get on board with the plan as well.

"Okay then, let's start getting ready!" Welf says, pounding his fist into his palm in an attempt to change the mood in the room.

That's the signal for everyone to plunge into preparations.

"This probably means we should join the hunting party from Rivira, right?" asks Ouka.

"Yeah. Even if we leave before them, the Dungeon is too big. Our chances of finding Lyu by searching randomly are miniscule," Lilly replies.

"We have no idea what floor she's on..." Chigusa agrees. Haruhime finishes the thought.

"So we use the power of the crowd and start by finding some leads as to where she is...?"

"Exactly, Lady Haruhime. But in order to reach Lady Lyu first, we'll have to get ahead of the hunting party at some point..." Mikoto responds.

Welf and Cassandra start inspecting our equipment, while some of the others begin packing for the search. I'm standing slightly to the side, watching over these encouraging preparations, when Aisha sidles up to me.

"Bell Cranell."

"Yes?"

"I think you know this, but the entire conversation that just happened was pure speculation. It's the interpretation that suits us—No, it's what suits you the best...It's entirely possible that elf killed the adventurer herself."

"..."

"Just make sure you remember that."

I feel like she knows something. Something about Lyu...Something about the current situation.

I gaze at the Amazon's back as she flips her long black hair. My heart is beating erratically.

"Great..." the girl muttered, pushing her glasses up with one finger.

Her pure-white mantle quivered. The light of a magic-stone lamp glinted gently off her aqua-blue hair. One section of her bangs was dyed snow white, and she held up a sharply glinting silver dagger in one hand.

As Asfi Al Andromeda peered around, her sandals decorated with golden wings chafed against the floor.

A cold draft floated past.

It was the distinctive chill of the subterranean dungeon, where not a speck of sunlight penetrated.

She wasn't in the "natural" dungeon that sprawled beneath Orario, however.

She was in Knossos, the man-made dungeon.

Asfi was leading *Hermes Familia* through the maze built by the cursed descendants of the legendary craftsman Daedalus.

"I thought this was going to be an easy job, sneaking along behind *Loki Familia* as they advanced through Knossos, checking out the paths they'd already cleaned up...but this place is crawling with monsters!"

The ground in front of Asfi and the others was strewn with the corpses of monsters that mere moments earlier had been locked in fierce battle. As if in response to Asfi's sigh, one of the bodies that had a crack in its magic stone dissolved into ash.

While *Hestia Familia* was gone on its expedition, some of the other familias were cooperating with the upper echelons of the Guild to secretly launch Operation Conquer Knossos. The Guild had probed into the man-made dungeon after the crimes of *Ikelos Familia*, headed by the brutal hunter Dix Perdix, brought its existence to light, eventually determining it wasn't something that could be ignored. So as not to raise the suspicions of the townsfolk, who were still recovering from the effects of the recent Xenos incident, the operation was being carried out on a top secret basis by a few select familias. *Hermes Familia* was one of them.

"I knew they were capturing the Xenos alive...but I didn't realize those *Ikelos Familia* guys were raising other monsters free-range. Or do you think they let them loose because they predicted we'd come down here?"

Asfi and the other members of the familia had been briefed about the Xenos by Hermes and were familiar with the whole situation.

As a result, they'd imagined a place where monsters from the Dungeon were being captured and kept. However, they hadn't expected to keep bumping into monsters every time they tried to advance down a path, exactly like in the real Dungeon. As she stood surrounded by the cold stone walls that made up the maze, Asfi let out three of her habitual sighs.

Something else was irritating her as well.

"Asfiiii! That masked elf has gone crazy! Wasn't she supposed to be backing us up?"

"Believe me—I'm aware..."

Lyu had been their lifeline, but now she was gone.

As the chienthrope girl screamed at her, Asfi grumbled at the long-gone elf.

"According to our agreement, you weren't supposed to act on your own...Right, Leon?"

The day before *Hestia Familia*'s operation to return the Xenos to the Dungeon began, Asfi had made Lyu Leon a promise.

"I've heard that the surviving Evils' Remnants are hiding out in Knossos. As soon as this situation is cleaned up, I'll search the dungeon and gather the information you want."

Later, Lyu had come to Asfi with a request.

"*I want to take part in your search,*" she'd said.

This request had been unexpected, but Asfi had been happy about it. There was no harm in bringing along extra forces if she had to go into that man-made dungeon with its shady past. All the better if it was Gale Wind.

Now that powerful helper had disappeared.

Plus, at Hermes's bidding, Aisha had joined up with Bell Cranell's group...If she had been here, things might have been different.

Aisha was a newcomer who, on paper, didn't yet belong to any faction and also happened to be *Hermes Familia*'s trump card.

Even if they were to make a mistake in Operation Conquer Knossos, her joining up with *Hestia Familia* would serve as insurance to make sure the boy and his party didn't get involved. But Aisha was Aisha, meaning she probably would have joined their expedition anyway, for the sake of Bell Cranell and her "little sister" from her former faction, *Ishtar Familia*.

Asfi stared into the blackness of the path down which Gale Wind had disappeared, pining after the impossible in spite of herself.

"I thought she'd calmed down...Did I simply underestimate her tenacity when it comes to the Evils?"

It had happened in an instant.

The moment Lyu glimpsed the group of adventurers attempting to escape at the far end of a passage filled with swarms of monsters, she had changed completely. Her sky-blue eyes had widened in fury while she emanated an air of intimidating bloodthirst that overwhelmed even Asfi. Then the elf chased after her fleeing targets without so much as a backward glance.

"It must have something to do with *Astrea Familia*'s history..."

Evils' Remnants lingered on in Knossos, even aside from the diabolical hunters.

These were the residual forces of the Evils who had brought an age of darkness to Orario and had been nearly wiped out five years earlier. Knossos suited them well as a hideout, for the Guild had been unable to capture them here.

Gale Wind's connection to these Evils was deep. She—Lyu Leon, member of the justice-seeking *Astrea Familia*—was undeniably tied to them.

The adventurers had fled in terror...Had her foe been among them?

"The flames of revenge are burning you, Leon...Will you succumb to them once again?"

No one was there to answer Asfi's mumbled question.

In the dim, man-made dungeon, she narrowed her eyes in pity.

CHAPTER 2
THE PROPHETESS OF TRAGEDY

A great calamity draws near.

The one who must not be approached is catastrophe incarnate. The one who must not be touched is the oracle of certain death.

A mother's lament shall call forth disaster, and despair shall let out its newborn cry.

The road of viscera shall be paved with the countless wails of the sacrificed.

The azure current shall run red with blood, and the grotesque horde shall rejoice.

The depths of hell shall overflow with corpses, returning all to the mother.

The squirrel shall bloom into flowers of flesh.

The fox shall be swiftly torn asunder.

The hammer shall be shattered.

The lives of the foreign warriors shall be as playthings.

The bloodied temptress shall abscond with a keepsake of the fox, but shall be mourned upon her defilement by countless fangs and claws.

A friend shall impart sorrow.

The fairy fated to guide all to ruin, compelling the roaring white flames, shall spin a cruel fate.

And so the cage of despair shall become a coffin, tormenting thyself.

Do not forget. Seek naught but the light of the reviving sun.

Gather the fragments, consecrate the flame, beseech the sun's light.

Take heed. Such is the banquet of calamity…

The dream was nothing special.

The mere product of the sleeping girl's fancy.

In short, it was simply a horrible nightmare, worse than any she had ever had before, so awful it made her physically ill. For the first time, the girl faced a divine message that was both undeniable and inescapable.

"——————————————————————————?!"

Cassandra jerked up in bed with a silent scream.

Straining so hard it seemed her vocal chords would burst, she felt enormous tears gathering at the corners of her panicked eyes.

"Huff…puff…huff…"

Her own ragged breaths reached her ears.

Her clothes were sopping with sweat, and she felt incredibly ill.

She stared ahead in a daze as if her eyes were glued in place, still heaving shallow breaths.

"What…just…happened?"

For a moment, confusion reigned.

In front of her, she saw bare stone walls. She was in Rivira, the traveler's town on the eighteenth floor. Outside, she could hear the bustle of adventurers like rippling waves. The wrinkled sheet spread around her belonged to a bed in a rented room.

As her consciousness returned, memories began to rise one after another.

Right…I laid down to rest before joining the hunting party…

Cassandra always took a nap before any big event.

Like a fortune-teller, the reason she did this was to dream.

Cassandra was endowed with the ability to have precognitive dreams.

In these dreams, vague images were accompanied by prophetic verses. Invariably, they hinted at impending disasters, and to Cassandra, they were as good as the future that awaited her. Although it was not a very pleasant experience, she made a point of always dreaming before any major event, because the import of her prophecies was so enormous. She'd done the same before *Apollo Familia* went on expeditions and before the War Game.

After Bell and the others decided to make contact with Gale Wind, Cassandra had obeyed the instinct throbbing in a corner of her brain and received permission to take a rest. She'd come alone to this room and lain down on the bed.

Judging by the hourglass in the room, less than an hour had passed since she'd lain down.

Next to the pillow lay several leaves of Argelica, an herb Cassandra always kept with her to ensure sound sleep.

"…What is going on…?"

Her head hurt, and she felt dizzy. Her lips would not stop trembling.

She had seen a nightmare. It had been absolutely terrible, incomparably worse than any dreams she had ever had on the surface.

It had been composed of seventeen prophecies accompanied by vivid, horrible scenes. A blackness embodying despair had crushed everything.

Crimson had gushed, intestines had spilled, and corpses had rolled.

Among them had been the bodies of Lilly, Haruhime, Welf, Mikoto, Chigusa, Ouka, Aisha, and also her friend Daphne.

The moment after she recalled the scene, a powerful nausea crawled up from her stomach.

"Blehhh!!"

She struggled to keep down the vomit rising in her throat. Failing in her attempt, she rolled off the bed and sprinted out of the room into the depths of the cave that had been turned into an inn. She forgot all about external appearances as she retched again and again into a pit carved in one of the walls. The taste of acid filled her throat.

When the nausea finally subsided, she reached her trembling hand out to the bucket beside her. Scooping up the pure water of the Under Resort that the innkeeper had hauled in, she rinsed her mouth repeatedly, then took several deep draughts.

I'm so cold...and so afraid...!

She thought back to when she had been very young, before she had joined *Apollo Familia.* Every time she had a scary dream back home, she would jump into her mother's bed, sobbing. She was filled with the desire to once again drown herself in the warm feeling of her mother's hands stroking her head and back. But her mother was not here. And even if she had been, the prophecies of the dream would not have disappeared.

That was because for Cassandra, they represented the waiting future.

"This is no good. Calm down...You have to think...If you don't think, the dream will come true...!"

Dream and reality raced through her mind, still entwined. She mulled over the visions.

The "fairy fated to guide all to ruin"...an elf? Gale Wind? The adventurers...Us...Will we be led by Gale Wind?...No, by chasing her, will we make the dream come true?

Gale Wind was an elf.

Cassandra knew that to be true based on information that had been shared five years ago when a bounty was placed on her head.

But she also seemed to be an acquaintance of Bell's and the others. More to the point, she was the masked adventurer who had taken part in the War Game against *Apollo Familia*.

And we're about to chase after Gale Wind to find out what really happened to the murdered adventurer...

That was their goal; that was the big picture.

But...

Is that the whole story...?

I don't know. I don't know. I don't know.

Is this really a straightforward murder investigation?

Just a story of helping out Bell's acquaintance?

Cassandra turned white as the memory of her prophetic dream assaulted her once again. Just then, she heard a voice nearby.

"Shit, that damn Bors, dazzled by money. Honestly, a hunting party to go after Gale Wind?...Huh? Hey, you, what are you doing over there?!"

Willy, the animal-person owner of the inn, had stumbled on Cassandra as he was carrying some packages into the back of the inn. And now that he had discovered her, he couldn't take his eyes off her.

Thanks to the sweat, her clothes were clinging to her body, outlining her womanly curves. The sight of a beautiful girl standing there exhausted and miserable stirred up the innkeeper's lust for conquest.

He gulped at this sexy view, but the next moment, he noticed the awful color of her face.

"Hey now, are you okay...? You look really pale...!"

"...I'm...fine."

Evading the man's concern, which bordered on panic, Cassandra stood up. Tottering like a baby, she walked forward and then broke into a run.

In an attempt to somehow distance herself from the scenes of her dream, she hurried toward Daphne and the others.

What I dreamed is not a future set in stone…!

Depending on Cassandra's actions, the future she foresaw could sometimes be avoided.

The party can still be saved!

She burst out of the cave, obsessed with that single, fervent desire.

"Mr. Welf, is the equipment all ready?" Lilly asked.

"Yes, and I've prepared the weapons for Bell and the rest as well. Some of the magic blades are still left, too. We can push into the lower levels once or twice more yet!" he answered.

"Since we need to get ahead of the other adventurers…our enemies won't necessarily just be monsters. We may have to fight other people as well. Don't forget that," Aisha added.

The party was already assembled in front of the inn. It was still night in the Dungeon, which explained why the light of white crystals illuminating their surroundings seemed to emit moonlight.

Lilly and Aisha were leading the group's final briefing.

"Hey, Cassandra! Where have you been? We're about to leave!!" Daphne shouted. Not only she but the rest of the party as well had noticed the girl had reappeared.

"Everyone!" she blurted out at the top of her lungs. As they fixed their eyes on her, she continued her entreaty. "About the hunting party…Is there any chance we can give up on it?"

"…Huh?"

"Something terrifying is going to happen…so…let's just not go…!"

Her voice was shaking. Welf and Lilly stared in disbelief at her crazy request. It was Daphne, of course, who rushed over to her first.

"Cassandra! Are you going to babble on again about some dream you had? Haven't I told you to get ahold of yourself?"

"…!"

Cassandra's old friend, whom she had known since their time

together in *Apollo Familia*, was turning a deaf ear to her pleas. Daphne never believed in her prophetic dreams. But it wasn't just Daphne. She couldn't get anyone to believe in them. It was like she was cursed. The exact same thing had happened during the War Game.

Lilly looked puzzled, and no one else seemed to believe her warning about "something terrifying" happening, either. Mikoto, Haruhime, and Chigusa looked confused, while Ouka had a dubious expression on his face, and Aisha seemed about to tell her that danger was just part of the package in the Dungeon.

In the past, no one believed me…but this time…!

Cassandra turned her desperate eyes from Daphne toward the white-haired boy.

"B-B-Bell…!"

There was one person who might believe her when no one else did.

The boy standing right in front of her, Bell Cranell.

Yes, she was sure of it; he was blessed with some kind of divine protection, something she might even call fate. Something strong enough to push aside Cassandra's curse. Ever since the day she had come to *Apollo Familia*'s former home in search of her lost pillow, this boy who believed what she said had been special to Cassandra.

He was also the party's leader, and now she turned her pleading eyes toward him.

A troubled look on his face, he slowly opened his mouth.

"I'm very sorry, Miss Cassandra…I can't."

Despair darkened her face.

"We have to meet up with Miss Lyu…I want to help her," he went on.

As he spoke, Cassandra caught the glint of his rubellite eyes, and she knew he meant what he said.

Aaah…It's no good. He's not going to give it up…!

Even if he did believe her warning, he was so overly kind that he would head toward the appointed place she had seen in her prophetic dream for the sake of the person he cared about.

For the first time, Cassandra understood that a firm will was synonymous with a strong destiny.

No matter what, she would not be able to stop the group.

The moment she realized this, the strength drained from her knees and she collapsed to the ground.

"Uh...Cassandra?"

As Lilly and the others gathered around in a panic, Daphne quickly supported her friend's limp form. She was about to ask if Cassandra was all right when she noticed just how pale her face was. From Daphne's perspective, Cassandra was always saying or doing something odd, and her appearance couldn't be called hearty even at its best, but she had never before seen her companion looking quite so haggard.

"...I'm sorry. I was planning to help search for Gale Wind..." Daphne said, still supporting Cassandra and looking around uncomfortably at the group. "But this girl seems to be feeling ill... Would you mind letting her rest a bit? I hate to ask this, but I'd like to stay here with her in Rivira—"

Just then, the slumping Cassandra opened her eyes wide.

"No!!"

"?!"

"No! Not that! Anything but that...!"

Lifting her face, Cassandra repeated her denial over and over as if she'd lost her mind. Not only Bell and the others but Daphne, too, was shocked. Gradually their surprise turned to deep confusion, and then they began to watch her as if she was a madwoman.

With both hands pressed to her head and her long hair disheveled, she felt her thin body shiver. Faced with her friends' failure to understand her message, she was the very picture of a prophetess of tragedy.

No matter what, I can't let myself be separated from them...!

Even if the general outline of her prophecy was inescapable, they could still avoid total destruction by stepping off the foretold path. And it was only Cassandra, who knew the content of the dream, who could help them to swerve from that path and onto another.

In other words, if Cassandra didn't go along with the party, the terrible calamity foretold in her dream was certain to befall them.

I can't; I can't…! There's no way I can abandon them now!

If Cassandra and Daphne stayed in town, they would definitely be safe. And not long ago, Cassandra would have chosen her own safety and that of her close friend over the group.

But it was too late. She'd been on an adventure with them, and she knew what kind of people they were.

Lilly was stingy when it came to money, but she was a prum who cared about her friends. Welf was a coolheaded metalsmith who not only took charge of their weapons but also took the lead in protecting the party. Ouka, Chigusa, and Mikoto were people she could respect for their strong sense of duty, characteristic of people from the Far East. Haruhime was kind and, in a way, similar to Cassandra herself; they had become close friends. Aisha she felt more awkward around, but she could still trust her as a steadfast older-sister figure.

And then there was Bell…who was special to her in so many ways.

"Miss Cassandra…Are you all right?"

Cassandra was aware that as he grew stronger and changed, she was gradually starting to see him differently. She was on the verge of tears knowing that even at this very moment, he was worrying about her.

There was no way she could abandon them now.

It's too late…

She looked around at Daphne and the others with a tired gaze. Last of all, her eyes rested on the white-haired boy.

"…I'm sorry I acted so selfishly…I'm going with you."

With that, the party—its enthusiasm temporarily dampened—regained its fighting spirit, albeit tinged with lingering suspicion. After a final check to make sure everything was ready, they headed out of town to meet up with the other adventurers in the hunting party.

As Cassandra joined the file, she privately reaffirmed her grim determination. She would save the party from the worst of fates as it marched toward ruin.

The rebellion of the unheeded prophetess had begun.
She alone would oppose the impeding ruin.

Nearly three hours had passed since the decision was made to form a hunting party and pursue Gale Wind. The adventurers had finished their preparations and were about to depart the eighteenth floor.

About half the party was made up of residents of Rivira and the remainder of adventurers who happened to be passing through at the time. Few had joined out of a sense of justice; the majority were hot-blooded fame seekers hoping to make a name for themselves by bringing down Gale Wind, the elf with a bounty on her head.

"If the information we have is accurate, Gale Wind is Level Four! And not just any Level Four, a top-class one! Rabbit Foot, Antianeira, I'm counting on you for this one, since you're the same level as she is. With you two, we should definitely be able to get this rebel under control," Bors said, bursting with confidence. They were gathered by the Central Tree, which led to the nineteenth floor.

Given his attitude, *Hestia Familia* was practically being forced to participate in the hunting party.

"Uh…yeah," Bell answered, breaking out in a sweat.

"Trust Bors to leave the work up to someone else," Lilly muttered, narrowing her eyes.

In reality, though, the situation was to their advantage. If they wanted to reach Lyu before anyone else, it would be easiest to obtain information from a position within the party's inner circle.

Luvis, Dormul, and the other members of *Modi Familia* and *Magni Familia* would stay behind in Rivira. They'd been in the lower levels far longer than *Hestia Familia*, and the extent of their exhaustion from prolonged torment at the hands of the enhanced moss huge was far greater than that of Bell and his companions. That went for their mental as well as their physical state. Staying behind was the natural decision.

Of course, it wouldn't have been surprising if Dormul's party of *Magni Familia* dwarfs had insisted on coming, given they'd boasted that "a little excursion like this is nothing for us."

But searching for and capturing anyone—not just Gale Wind—in the sprawling Dungeon was a tall order indeed. And compared to the floors of the upper levels, those below the nineteenth floor were truly enormous. The fact that parties sent on quests for missing adventurers typically failed to find even a single trace, let alone their actual remains, only showed how difficult any search would be. And this time, neither the goal nor the destination of the missing individual was known. The hunting expedition was expected to last quite a few days. Copious amounts of food had been taken from the town's stocks and packed for the large party.

"Keep your eyes peeled for any sign of the fugitive! If you meet with other adventurers, ask them for information! Animal people, this is your chance to show off those noses you're so proud of!"

Bors had ordered the party to search each floor as thoroughly as possible and, when they were done, to post sentries at the passageways that connected one floor to the next. So long as they occupied the lone route leading to the upper floors, their prey was sure to fall into their net eventually. And so the hunting party set forth, leaving behind a guard ample enough that even a Level 4 adventurer could not easily defeat it, and headed toward the lower levels with many second-tier adventurers.

"So after we search every corner of each floor, we post guards at the entrances and exits…Sounds to me like the standard formula for searching this insanely huge Dungeon," Aisha said.

The group had made it to the Colossal Tree Labyrinth on the twenty-first floor. As the adventurers rested in a large room, she, Lilly, and Ouka were chatting and checking their weapons and items.

"It's the kind of strategy that relies completely on manpower. I wonder if Bors is wrong in choosing it," Lilly said.

"In other words, you think the head of Rogue Town might just be grandstanding," Ouka replied.

The party led by *Hestia Familia* was sitting together in a field of flowers near the center of the room, where it would be harder for monsters to catch them by surprise.

"Even if the method itself isn't bad, do you really think we're going to find Gale Wind by moving around in such a big group? Usually in searches, people split up into smaller groups...I'm betting that before we have a chance to slip away, this big pack is going to disintegrate."

The more adventurers in a party, the more frequent their encounters with monsters. Acquaintances might help one another, but predictably, the proudly confident upper-class adventurers had so far been fighting independently, without much care for cooperation. The members of the party were constantly cursing and yelling at one another, and even the supporters could be seen pulling spare weapons from their packs to sell in exchange for magic stones and drop items.

Twirling her baton-like dagger, Daphne watched from a distance as several adventurers fought over the spring water bubbling from another corner of the room. She sighed.

"Well, if that makes things easier for us, there's no harm in it. Still...I wonder how deep that tavern elf has burrowed," Welf said.

"So far, we haven't seen the slightest trace of Lady Lyu..." Mikoto answered.

"She seems to have been chasing someone...And given that she's Level Four, she'll have no problem delving into the lower levels..." Chigusa added.

Already, half a day had passed since the hunting party set out. Lilly checked the broken watch around her neck.

"For future reference, let's not take on any search quests. They just don't make financial sense," she murmured, shrugging her narrow shoulders. Haruhime and Bell smiled wryly.

"..."

Of the group, only Cassandra had a strained expression on her face. She was lost in thought, failing completely to take advantage of the precious rest time to relax.

That dream represents the worst possible outcome...If the prophecy comes true, then this party is done for. In order to avoid that, I have to decipher this oracle...!

She was turning the words of her dream over and over in her mind, trying to guess what they might mean.

In the past, when people hadn't listened to her prophecies, she had either given up or just kept muttering about the inevitable future. Now she was desperately searching for a way out.

"A great calamity"..."catastrophe incarnate"..."a mother's lament shall call forth disaster"...I'm guessing that calamity, catastrophe incarnate, and disaster are supposed to be synonyms...

Most of the time, the first part of Cassandra's prophetic dreams gave an outline of the future. And inevitably, that future was *something inevitable* that Cassandra could not interfere with.

I'm sure "mother" must refer to the Dungeon. The Dungeon is the mother of monsters, *as they say in Orario. If that's the case, then considering the phrase "newborn cry"...the disaster the mother will call forth must be a monster or monsters that will be spawned.*

Cassandra hugged her chest tightly through her battle clothes.

The bloodshed will begin when despair lets out its newborn cry. "Countless wails of the sacrificed," "the road of viscera," "the azure current shall run red with blood"...Going by my past prophetic dreams, these vivid words almost certainly hint at death...but is it us adventurers chasing after "the fairy fated to guide all to ruin" who will die?

In other words, did the prophecy mean that the Dungeon would spawn one or more powerful monsters that would claim many victims? That interpretation was probably the most accurate. Up to this point, the reasoning was straightforward.

But what will the powerful monsters be like? Will something even worse than that enhanced moss huge appear in the Dungeon? Something strong enough to kill us all—even Aisha, who's second-tier?

"*The squirrel shall bloom into flowers of flesh*"...In her dream, Lilly had died with her guts spilled everywhere.

"*The fox shall be swiftly torn asunder*"...Haruhime had been drowning in a sea of blood, torn to pieces.

"*The hammer shall be shattered*"...Welf had lost his arms and legs, a cruel vision.

"*The lives of the foreign warriors shall be as playthings*"...The bodies of Mikoto, Chigusa, and Ouka had been piled atop one another.

"*The bloodied temptress shall abscond with a keepsake of the fox, but shall be mourned upon her defilement by countless fangs and claws*"...Aisha, carrying the body of the renart, had lagged with exhaustion before eventually getting swarmed and then devoured by hordes of monsters.

"Urgh...?!"

As the words and images of each line of the prophecy rose before her mind's eye, Cassandra hurriedly pressed a hand to her mouth.

Although the images were hazy, like those of a daydream, the visions of her companions being cruelly murdered were nevertheless overwhelmingly gruesome and horrifying. She still could not shake off the shock of seeing them.

Least of all...

Daphne!

"*A friend shall impart sorrow.*" In her dream, a blood-drenched, hollow-eyed Daphne drew her last breath before Cassandra's eyes.

Cassandra felt the tears coming, but she desperately held them back. That wasn't reality. She needed to fight now to ensure that this tragedy did not befall Daphne and the others.

Calm down; calm down!

She had no time to cry or despair. She scolded herself angrily.

As long as you're sitting around dreaming, Aisha and everyone else are going to be slaughtered. But what monster could do something like that?...A floor boss?

Regaining control of her emotions, Cassandra surveyed the large room once again. It was full of well-armed upper-class adventurers. At a glance, she guessed there must be around seventy of them. The only monster she could imagine massacring a group like this was a Monster Rex.

"...Uh, Miss Lilly? Do you think the floor boss, um...is going to spawn soon?"

"You mean the Amphisbaena? Don't underestimate me, Miss Cassandra! I went to the Guild and researched when it appears specifically to make sure we wouldn't bump into it on this expedition. One was most recently taken down just about two weeks ago, so we still have another two weeks before it appears again!"

"R-right..." Cassandra said, lowering her head in embarrassment as Lilly scolded her angrily; after all, fighting a floor boss on one's first expedition was no joke.

"The Amphisbaena is a lower-level floor boss, right? I'm sure I heard that it appears on the twenty-seventh floor," Welf said.

"Lady Aisha, did you ever fight one when you were with *Ishtar Familia*?" Mikoto asked.

"Yeah. They're stronger than Goliath for sure. The Guild rates them at Level Six because they live in the water, but their raw ability is closer to a Five. If we encountered one with this many upper-class adventurers in our group, we'd be able to take it down," she answered.

As Cassandra listened in on their conversation, she found herself worrying once again.

So Aisha's already fought a lower-level Monster Rex...If what she says is true, then a Monster Rex definitely wouldn't be able to cause the kind of massacre I saw in my dream...

With this thought, she grew less and less sure of what the coming calamity would be. Her head began to ache.

Are there going to be multiple monsters? A huge monster party or something like that...?

It was possible. Still, she felt that wasn't quite right.

After thinking for a long while, she shook her head. She wasn't getting anywhere trying to figure out what the exact nature of the calamity would be. Resigning herself to the fact that further guessing would be futile, she moved on to thinking about another verse of the prophecy.

The only warning in this dream was in the line about the "reviving sun"...But what does "the sun" mean...?

Sometimes, Cassandra's dreams contained warnings about how to avoid the prophecy. Usually, they were abstract or allegorical and therefore hard to interpret. As a result, Cassandra typically was unable to avoid mishap.

What is the sun a symbol or allegory for? Maybe Apollo? Will something connected with him save "thyself"—me—when I get shut up in the "coffin"? Or is the sun a reference to time? Will something happen during the daytime? But time in the Dungeon is different from time on the surface...Argh! This is going nowhere!

She banged her head with her fist, then sank into depression. Haruhime and Chigusa drew back in surprise. Meanwhile, Daphne—who had known Cassandra long enough to grow used to her moods—seemed fed up.

"Gather the fragments, consecrate the flame, beseech the sun's light"...It seems like this line is connected to the one about the "sun," but I don't know how it connects to what comes before or after...

Cassandra tightened the hand resting on her knee into a fist.

I have a feeling I know where the massacre is going to take place...If we can just avoid winding up there at the appointed time, we should be able to avoid the "banquet of calamity"...

Cassandra breathed in the distinctive scent released by the Dungeon flowers as she mulled over this conclusion, thinking of what she could do.

"Uh, Miss Cassandra?"

She hadn't even noticed that the white-haired boy was kneeling in front of her, peering into her face.

"Oh! Ack! Mr. Bell!"

Bell smiled wryly at her as she squealed in surprise. He hesitated for a moment, then slowly opened his mouth.

"Um…If something is worrying you, please tell me."

"Huh?"

"I know we're from different familias, but we're in this party together, and…Well, if there's anything I can do, I'd like to help. I mean, it doesn't have to be me; it could be Miss Daphne or Miss Haruhime…"

He handed her a cool water bottle. It seemed he'd braved the quarrelling adventurers to draw fresh water from the spring. He'd noticed Cassandra's troubled face and wanted to do something for her.

Most likely, he had noticed she was disturbed by the prophetic dream even before they left Rivira.

Cassandra blinked in surprise and blushed.

He's really…changed…

Not long ago, he'd blushed all the time and gotten into a fluster whenever something happened. Just like Cassandra herself.

During the expedition, Mikoto had taught her a proverb from the Far East, using Bell as an example: "If you haven't seen a man for three days, watch closely when you meet." It really was true—his skills seemed to grow day by day. He'd become a true leader for the party.

Of course, he still wasn't what she'd call "dignified," but whenever he noticed something was wrong, he thought about what he could do to help, then acted on it. That was true with the moss huge, when she'd been unsure what to do as a healer about the parasitic vines plaguing the party. He'd sat beside her and held her hand, encouraging her.

It seemed she could still feel the warmth of his grip.

When she thought about the fact that he was younger than her on top of it all, she wanted to cry.

"Thank…you…" she said softly, taking the bottle and bringing it to her lips for a noisy gulp.

He scratched his cheek and smiled shyly.

Cassandra didn't know what had happened to make him change so much. But she felt like she could drown in his kindness.

"Uh, um..."

She had just opened her mouth to say something, still unsure what that something would be, when an uproar arose over by the door to the room.

"Bors! It's a herd of mammoth fools!" an adventurer shouted.

Although the size of the creatures varied by individual, all measured between six and seven meders at the withers and were imposing even at a distance. Their gently curving, upturned tusks were as long as spears, and their fur was as red as blood.

Mammoth fools were a rare instance of a monster in the Colossal Tree Labyrinth whose danger came simply from brute strength; most others had special abilities like irregular attacks or hard insect-like carapaces. The mammoths were also the largest of the ordinary middle-level monsters.

"A bunch of large-category guys, eh? Get ready for a fight, you lot! Rabbit Foot, you too!"

Called out by name by the ax-wielding Bors, Bell hopped to like a veritable rabbit. By the time Cassandra let out a sigh, he was already far away, leading the charge toward the herd of monsters.

"..."

Aisha and Ouka rushed to join the battle against the four mammoth fools, whom they seemed to view as a mere hassle, and Chigusa ran off to support them. Cassandra gazed sadly at Bell as he fought.

He'd received a broadsword from Bors and was slicing the beasts around their legs, bringing them to the ground with a deafening crash. As he wielded his magical flames, the courageous boy looked to Cassandra just like a fairy-tale hero.

He was the only one who wasn't clearly marked for death in my dream...

"The fairy fated to guide all to ruin, compelling the roaring white flames, shall spin a cruel fate."

The "roaring white flames" were the only words that seemed to refer to Bell.

Cassandra was sure "the fated fairy" was Lyu. It was unavoidable destiny that these two would cross paths. The sinister part was how the fairy had been *compelling* the flames. It seemed to be a prophecy of a different type from that foretold for Aisha and the others.

She had seen a small fairy flapping her wings as roaring white flames surrounded her. The vision had ended just before she was engulfed by some kind of jet-black catastrophe.

If anyone was going to overturn this horrible prophecy—wouldn't it be him?

Cassandra pursed her lips. Mikoto, Daphne, and Welf had stayed behind to protect the supporters and watch for other monsters; now, taking the first step toward combatting the prophecy, Cassandra approached Welf.

"Um, Mr. Crozzo."

The young smith had been watching the battle and was about to join in.

"Stop calling me by my family name, would you? Welf is fine," he said, looking disappointed to have been interrupted on his way to fight.

At the same time, he was slightly surprised that Cassandra had called out to him. She apologized in a fluster and steeled herself to bring up the topic at hand. She had decided to ask the High Smith—whose skills had been steadily improving—for a favor.

When she did, he answered frankly, as was his nature as a craftsman.

"...I can do it, but why are you asking me all of a sudden?"

"Uh, um..."

"Honestly, I can't say I'm eager to do it. We've decided that he'll only carry weapons I've forged myself."

The naturally shy Cassandra seemed on the verge of retreating in response to his words, but then she pursed her lips again.

"He...Mr. Bell can be reckless for the sake of other people...That's the kind of person he is. I want to help him..." she said, looking the smith in the eye.

She didn't mention her dream. She knew he wouldn't believe her if she did. But he just might believe an admission of her honest feelings.

Like Bell, Cassandra had changed and grown. Welf listened silently as she spoke, a fierce glint in her timid downward-slanting eyes. He paused for a moment, then turned up the corners of his mouth.

"Okay. I'll do it."

"R-r-really?"

"Yup. Never mind the ramblings of a prideful smith. It's just like with the magic blades...I've decided to stop weighing my pride against my friends," he said, smiling as if he'd put the past behind him.

Somehow, Cassandra could tell that his smile was the result of a long inner struggle. She was so envious of him that she was momentarily speechless, and at the same time she sympathized with that struggle.

"Plus, something about this current business seems fishy to me. I agree with you that Bell seems likely to do something reckless. I wouldn't be surprised if he turned every adventurer in this room against him in order to protect that elf...After all, my partner in crime has a record of doing stuff like that."

He'd been thinking about the time with the Xenos, a serious expression on his face, but to hide his true thoughts, he ended on a joke. Cassandra bobbed her head energetically.

"Th-th-thank you so much!"

For the first time, she felt as if her actions would have some impact on the future. Nothing whatsoever had changed with regard to the outcome of her dream, but still, she felt extremely happy.

"Li'l E, bring me that portable forge I brought along. And lend me that thing of yours while you're at it. It's probably dragging on the ground because it's too long."

"But Mr. Welf, you took the measurements yourself!"

Welf retrieved the tools from Lilly, whose temper had flared once again. Setting the box-shaped forge in front of him, he began constructing a miniature workshop in one corner of the Dungeon.

"You girls, give me a hand already. Monsters are gathering, and it seems like Bell and the others are going to be a while. I'd like to get this done before they finish."

"Yes, sir!"

Mikoto, Haruhime, and Daphne gathered beside the smith to help. The other adventurers who had remained in the rear guard drew around, too, craning their necks as the work began.

As the cries of the fighting adventurers and monsters echoed in the background, Cassandra realized she was feeling excited.

"Ahhh..."

Hestia let out a relaxed sigh and lay her chest against the table, squashing her ample breasts.

She was in the *Hestia Familia* home, Hearthstone Manor, lazing around the living room.

"You seem pretty sluggish today. Do you have the day off work?" Miach asked. He'd come over with some packages.

"Yeah. By some miracle, I'm off from Hephaistos's place and Jyaga Maru Kun, too. But I hate to waste a day off when Bell and the others aren't around!" Hestia replied.

With the multi-familia-faction alliance off on the expedition and the entirety of *Hestia Familia* taking part, their home was left defenseless. To compensate, several deities Hestia was close with were taking turns dispatching familia members to Hearthstone Manor. Today was *Miach Familia*'s turn. Miach himself had come along, and as he chatted with Hestia, the chienthrope Nahza opened the door and walked in.

"Lady Hestia, I cleaned up a bit..."

"Oh wow, you did, really? Thanks so much!"

"It's no trouble...After all, you're making dinner for me and letting me take a bath here, too."

"Well, that's sweet of you to put it that way," Hestia said.

Nahza smiled, her eyelids drooping so that at first glance she looked sleepy. The tail swooping down from her waist was swinging back and forth, too, as if she was looking forward to the evening.

"By the way, Hestia, what's that racket out in the backyard?" Miach asked.

"Oh, that...Hephaistos sent over one of her young smiths as a guard, but he's an odd one. He asked to have a look at Welf's workshop, given they used to be in the same familia...and when I said it was okay, he ransacked the place, and now he seems to have started making a weapon of some sort..."

"Well in that case, I'd like to have a look around Lilliluka's room... I bet she has some unusual items and medicines hidden in there...Is that all right with you?" Nahza asked.

"Give me a break! She would be furious with me!"

Miach smiled wryly at Hestia's evident low position, despite the fact that she was a goddess.

"Are you feeling nervous with Bell and the others gone?"

"Yeah, of course I am. But I still have to be ready to give them a proper welcome when they come back, like I'm happy about it all," Hestia replied before asking Miach a question in return. "What about you? It was Daphne and Cassandra who went on the expedition, right?"

"It goes without saying that I can't stop worrying and I'm lonely... But up till recently, it's always been just Nahza and me. It's weird to say that things are back to how they were, but I'm treating it like a little reward for myself and having a rather peaceful interlude."

"..."

"We've known each other for so long. I feel the most at ease with Nahza by my side," Miach said pleasantly, a handsome god's smile on his face.

A loud clatter came from the shelf that Nahza had been tidying up, her back to the two deities. Her tail was wagging furiously.

Hestia had no idea what the backstory was behind Miach's affectionate words, but for some reason it made her chest burn, so she forcefully changed the subject.

"Anyway, Miach…I wanted to ask you about Cassandra," she said, her face and tone docile. "I've been thinking this since she was with Apollo, but…"

"Yes…She can see things. Things even we deities can't see."

Nahza turned toward the two deities, who were nodding at each other, and tilted her head quizzically.

"I don't know what Apollo was up to by keeping her in his familia…but she seems to carry the mysteries of the mortal realm within her."

"Mysteries that are beyond even us…I do understand why the deities have been so fascinated by the mortal plane ever since their first descent from the heavens," Hestia said, leaning her weight against the back of the chair. For a moment, she stared up toward the ceiling, as if she was reflecting on the very nature of the mortal plane.

"I haven't talked with her much myself. What kind of a girl is she anyway?" she asked, as if the question had just occurred to her.

"Cassandra is a strange one…" Nahza replied, taking a teakettle from the shelf. As she talked, she went about preparing some black tea for the group. "At first she was like Bell—No, even more timid and nervous than he is…Lately I think she's become attached to us…But she's always waxing philosophical about things…"

"Philosophical?" Hestia asked.

"I can't really explain it…But I think it has to do with destiny or something like that…"

"Ah, destiny…"

"She says things that are obviously lies, and sometimes I really don't get her…Like when my favorite cup broke, for some reason she was more upset than anyone…"

As Nahza and Hestia talked, Miach stood to the side, listening quietly.

"That's what I mean about her being an odd one. It's like she's living in a different world from the rest of us…" Nahza said.

"…"

"And Daphne being Daphne, she says exactly what she's thinking, and that makes Cassandra even less confident and more timid than ever..."

Nahza sniffed at the steam rising from the kettle before continuing with a smile.

"Still, I like them. They're what the gods might call an 'odd couple.' She's always worrying about something, always looking gloomy..."

"I did notice that she seemed a bit on the dismal side...But what's your takeaway, Nahza?"

"She does cheer up when she sees Bell..."

"Wh-wh-what?! No way! Don't tell me even that girl is scheming after him?!" Hestia said, leaping up with a clatter in response to Nahza's expression of what she had sensed with her female instincts.

"I don't think that's the case," the chienthrope said as she set three cups of tea on the table. "I'm surprised that she's continued as an adventurer this far."

"Despite her appearance, she seems to have strength at her core. Sometimes when she smiles, she looks so full of light even I can't take my eyes off her," Miach said.

"..."

"Ouch, Nahza! What are you pinching me for? That hurts...!"

"I don't think you should be talking about 'not being able to take your eyes off' anyone!"

As this comic dialogue between members of *Miach Familia* unfolded, Hestia munched absently on the pieces of Jyaga Maru Kun she'd brought out to go with the tea, looking completely uninterested.

"...Oh, is someone at the door?"

The sound of the doorbell echoed through the room.

"I'll get it," Nahza said, standing up.

She returned a moment later with a letter in her hand.

"It seems to be a letter from Lilliluka...She says they've been asked to do something on the eighteenth floor..."

"A letter from my supporter? It's hard to believe that little miser would spend the money to send me something..."

Usually, if someone was asked by fellow adventurers to take on a quest while already in the Dungeon, they requested compensation above the market rate. In other words, they took advantage of the situation. That was all the truer of upper-class adventurers with the ability to make it as far as a safety point. Hestia had spoken jokingly, but the fact that Lilly—who was a notoriously strict financial manager—had gone as far as using the familia emblem and writing up a signed and sealed deed, and moreover that she had sent a messenger from the eighteenth floor when Bell could have made the trip himself, gave her a bad feeling.

"...A hunting party has formed to chase down that tavern elf?! And in order to do something about it, they're joining the hunting party?!"

"Hestia, what's going on?" Miach asked.

"I—I—I have no clue..."

Hestia was in shock over the unexpected news in the letter. It was written cryptically so that nothing would be given away if it was intercepted by someone outside the familia, but it mentioned their encounter with the enhanced species and their decision to end the expedition.

Hestia reread the letter two or three times, then handed it to Miach, dumbfounded.

"What in the world is going on down in the Dungeon...?"

All Hestia could do was sigh at the last line, in which Lilly requested that she send support troops into the Dungeon in case something happened—in case Lyu was caught—in order to free her.

Despite the attack by the mammoth fools while they rested, the hunting party for Gale Wind moved on without incident. As Bors instructed, they searched each floor, then posted guards at the inter-floor passageways. Soon they had arrived at the twenty-fourth floor.

A day had passed, and even the adventurers who had been most enthusiastic about chasing down the famed fugitive were now beginning to lag.

"Hey, stop crawling along! Let's hurry it up! Gale Wind could commit another crime!"

"Calm down, Turk. It's way stupider to rush forward and miss clues on the way. I can't deny I'm feeling slow, though..."

In the distance, Cassandra could hear adventurers squabbling over how to proceed. She turned to Lilly.

"Um, Miss Lilly...Can you lend me the floor map?"

"What, again?"

"Yes, I'd like to see the one for a different floor this time...Sorry."

Lilly narrowed her round chestnut-brown eyes suspiciously but nevertheless withdrew the floor map from her backpack.

Cassandra, who was already holding the other one, took it from her.

"Whatever could Lady Cassandra be up to...?"

"Y-y-yes, what could it be? She keeps on looking at the Dungeon maps..."

Haruhime and Chigusa whispered to each other as Cassandra tucked her healer's wand under one arm and peered at the unfurled parchment. Cassandra didn't notice them; she was completely absorbed in the map. A drop of sweat fell from her tense face.

"Watch out, Cassandra; you're going to trip," Daphne said, scanning the path ahead of them.

Cassandra had tried to stop Bors and his companions from moving ahead with the hunting expedition, but she had failed, as she had expected. Resigned to the fact that she would have to do something herself, she was now completely fixated on preventing the prophecy from unfolding. In order to do so, she was attempting to memorize as much information about each floor as she could.

Staring down at the map in her hands so hard she practically burned a hole through it, she racked her brain for some new idea.

"I knew this would be a long process, but the search is really taking time, isn't it...?"

"We're almost done with the middle levels, though. If Lady Lyu is in the Colossal Tree Labyrinth, you'd think we'd find at least one or two signs fairly soon..."

Cassandra listened as Mikoto and Lilly chatted, and in her heart, she shook her head.

No...That's not right.

Gale Wind wasn't in this part of the Dungeon.

This was not where "fairy" was fated to guide her pursuers to ruin. The prophetess of tragedy knew in her heart that the Colossal Tree Labyrinth was not the appointed place of catastrophe.

The nightmarish prophetic dream had murmured as much to her.

"The azure current shall run red with blood, and the grotesque horde shall rejoice.

"The depths of hell shall overflow with corpses, returning all to the mother."

Three out of the prophecy's seventeen verses mention places, and the fifth and sixth verses of the first half mention specific locations...!

"The azure current."

"The depths of hell."

In the context of what was going on, there was only one place these lines could be referring to.

Yes! In other words—

"Huh? An explosion?!"

"The shock waves are coming from below...From the lower levels?!"

—It could only be the Water Capital.

The trembling ground and sound of something cracking threw the adventurers into disarray.

The map of the lower levels that Cassandra still gripped trembled as she held her breath.

She knew that "the time" had come.

The starting whistle had blown, and now the prophecy would begin to unfold.

Her lips trembled silently.

"Get going!"

At Bors's command, everyone began to run. The adventurers licking their chops in anticipation and Bell's tension-riddled party alike were drawn forward by the intermittent sounds of explosions. Cassandra, running at the back of the group, was tormented by an anxiety unlike any she had ever experienced. Desperately, she tried to calm her thumping heart.

As they rushed through the passageway connecting the twenty-fourth and twenty-fifth floors, countless footsteps echoed down the crystal-encrusted cave. Reaching the end of the long slope, they leaped toward the mouth of the cave, which was flooded with blue light.

Before them flowed the gorgeous emerald-blue water of the Great Falls and the yawning crystalline cavern.

For the second time, Bell and the rest of his party found themselves gazing out at the magnificent scene of the New World.

"Whoa...Another explosion!"

"Is Gale Wind on a rampage?"

"The shock waves are coming from farther below...Could the source be the twenty-seventh floor?"

The Water Capital began on the twenty-fifth floor and continued to the twenty-seventh, with the Great Falls connecting all three floors. On each of these floors, a massive cavern contained the falls and a plunge pool as huge as a lake. Far, far below the cliff's edge where they stood now was the end point on the twenty-seventh floor. Surrounded by adventurers, Bors squinted down at it with his right eye, the one without the patch.

Gray smoke distinct from the waterfall's mist drifted upward as a crystal column sank into the plunge pool like a calved iceberg, broken off by the shock waves. He could just make it out through the masses of spray that billowed up in a white mist from the falls.

"Those explosions don't sound like they were made by monsters! Ten to one, this is the work of an adventurer—or to put more of a point on it, Gale Wind! I'm going to choose the best of you to go down to the twenty-seventh floor! The rest of you, stay here and guard the passageway!"

"Yaaaaaah!"

In response to Bors's words, the adventurers enthusiastically thrust their swords, spears, and axes into the air. Their lethargy now vanished, the mercenary bunch of rogues shouted spirited battle cries as the hunt for Gale Wind finally began.

Meanwhile, Bell's party swiftly formed a circle a few steps away and began discussing their strategy.

"This is where things get critical. We've got to find Lyu before the other adventurers," Lilly said.

"Yeah. We'll need to get information from them about what's happening, too," Bell added.

"Clearly...But what were those explosions? They felt strong. Do you really think the elf is using her magic or something?" Welf asked.

Cassandra had been ignoring their conversation and instead glancing nervously back toward the passage to the twenty-fourth floor, but now she shook her head. It was time to sever ties with the part of her that still wanted to turn back.

Even within her eighteen short years, she had had enough painful experiences to know that a weak impulse like that would do nothing to avert her prophetic dream.

Now was when it all began.

From here on, she could make no mistakes if she was going to avert the prophecy. That was what she told herself, trying to gain courage even as her pounding heart made her feel like vomiting again.

"So, moving on...Lilly has a funny feeling about the twenty-seventh floor. We somehow need to join the special party and make contact with Ly—"

"Uh, wait!"

Cassandra interrupted the party's prum leader mid-sentence.

"I don't think we need to go to the twenty-seventh floor, do we...? It would be hard to move around in such a large group..."

There was much she didn't understand about her prophetic dream, but at least she had a good idea of the location.

"The depths of hell shall overflow with corpses, returning all to the mother."

Cassandra had deduced that "the depths of hell" referred to the end point of the Great Falls on the twenty-seventh floor, which was the lowest level of the Water Capital. In other words, that was where the catastrophe was going to happen.

If only they could stay off the twenty-seventh floor, Lilly and the others should be able to avoid the foretold death. For Cassandra, who had wrestled with the meaning of many nonsensical dreams in the past, that one point seemed certain. As she inwardly reproached herself for speaking so incoherently, Daphne spoke up next to her.

"I agree with Cassandra. Even if we've fought on this floor before, we've only explored it once. Don't you think we're most likely to slip up in a place we're totally unfamiliar with?"

"D-D-Daphne..."

"Even if we rely on Rabbit Foot and Antianeira for protection, I doubt we'll be able to find her faster than the other adventurers."

Daphne's reasoning was totally unconnected to what Cassandra was concerned about—avoiding the prophecy. But Daphne had been pushed into the role of commander in *Apollo Familia*, and she wasn't about to give up her cautious attitude toward a risky area like the lower levels.

"Anyway, I personally don't want to risk my life for someone I barely know," she concluded jokingly.

"...I see. You're right that speed is inversely related to the size of the party, and this time we need to move fast. Therefore, let's not send everyone to the twenty-seventh floor," Lilly said, taking her mentor's words into consideration.

Cassandra felt incredibly relieved. She was sure they had avoided the worst scenario. She let the tension drain from her shoulders and sighed.

"So in addition to Mr. Bell and Miss Aisha, who should go?"

Instantly, Cassandra's body seized up again.

"Aaaaaah, ummmm?!"

She interrupted Lilly again, raising her right hand. Aisha, whose death had been clearly foretold in the prophecy, must not be allowed to go to the twenty-seventh floor. She had to stop her!

Lilly looked fed up at yet another interruption, while Aisha glanced at her suspiciously. Cassandra, who had not thought in advance about what she was going to say, moved her mouth silently, then finally squeezed out a few words.

"M-M-Miss Aisha should stay on the twenty-fifth floor with everyone else..."

"Why?"

"Uh...The other day when Haruhime suffered a Mind Down and I had to carry her to the eighteenth floor...she was actually really heavy...!"

"Huh?!"

It was a lie.

She was extremely light.

The Goliath Robe felt heavier than Haruhime. In fact, although her chest was large, her hips were so slight it made Cassandra feel hopeless about her own form. She flinched and blushed as the renart yelped defensively at the false claims.

"In case we have to escape and she has to be carried again, I just, um, have a feeling that Lilly and I might not be able to do it by ourselves...O-o-of course everyone else will protect us, too, but without Aisha here, what will we do about Miss Haruhime, since she's so heavy...?"

As Cassandra frantically repeated the word *heavy*, Daphne gave her a look that said, *Do you have a grudge against her or something?*

Meanwhile, tears were welling in Haruhime's eyes as the others talked about her like a piece of luggage. She kept glancing at Bell, who seemed not to know what expression to arrange his face into and looked on the verge of fainting from embarrassment.

"...Well, it's true that she's grown a lot since we were in the Far East. Especially her chest," Ouka mumbled.

"Really?" Welf answered with a bit too much curiosity.

"Honestly, Ouka!! And Welf, too!" Chigusa snapped, spreading the chaos still further through the group. Mikoto, who had been standing by, nervous and unsure what to do, rubbed Haruhime's shoulder comfortingly.

The renart's sniffles disappeared into the thundering of the Great Falls.

"Who cares if this silly fox is light or heavy? All she has to do is stand here by the passageway. There are plenty of other adventurers around, and if things get really dangerous, she can always use her magic," Aisha said.

"Uh..."

"You guys really demand a lot of care. To tell you the truth, if you don't learn to fend for yourselves when I'm not around, I don't know what I'm going to do. That goes for *Hestia Familia* as well."

Cassandra didn't know how to respond to Aisha's extremely straightforward words. At the same time, seeing Aisha's genuine concern for her "little sister," Cassandra felt ashamed at her thoughtless attempt to use Haruhime for her own ends.

Still, she had to find some way of preventing Aisha from going to the twenty-seventh floor. She was growing more and more distressed.

"...Um, Miss Aisha."

Bell had been staring at Aisha's face, and finally he spoke up.

"Would you mind doing as Cassandra asked and staying on the twenty-fifth floor?"

"Huh...?" Cassandra gasped. She watched in surprise as Bell continued.

"What are you talking about, kid? Don't tell me you're going to ask me to watch over that dumb fox, too?"

"I'd be lying if I said that wasn't part of it...But there's someone else I want you to keep an eye on."

"Someone you want me to keep an eye on?" Aisha echoed doubtfully.

Bell leaned in closer to the group and pointed at one of the other adventurers.

"That werewolf who's been insisting it was Lyu…Gale Wind… who committed the murder. He kept repeating it over and over, like he was trying to fire everyone up."

"…Now that you mention it, he was urging everyone to hurry the whole way here. When I think about it, it does seem a bit unnatural," Lilly said.

"Exactly. I think that guy is…lying."

Lilly and the others glanced furtively toward the group of adventurers, where they could glimpse the werewolf talking and linking arms with the others.

Bell watched him for a moment, then looked back at Aisha.

"If Lyu is innocent, then that guy is up to no good."

"…"

"If he does anything fishy, I want you to stop him…Or am I off the mark?"

Although Bell had been sharing his thoughts without hesitation up to this point, he ended on a less-than-confident note.

Instead of directly answering his question as to whether his assessment was off, Aisha let out a long sigh.

"There may be some truth to what you say. Just to be safe, you and I should split up," she said.

"All right then, Miss Aisha, I'm counting on you."

"But. If my sense of things is right…that elf will be too much for you to handle on your own," Aisha said, looking Bell over sharply. She seemed to know something the others didn't.

Bell recoiled for an instant, but then his face took on a resolute expression.

"I believe in Miss Lyu."

"…Do as you like, then." Aisha sighed, narrowing her eyes and tacitly accepting that she would stay behind on the twenty-fifth floor.

Cassandra watched in shock as Bell thanked the Amazon. His rubellite eyes met hers for a moment, and his mouth curved into a faintly wry smile.

Aha...

She realized that Bell had seen her desperately trying to keep Aisha on this floor and had extended a helping hand. Of course, he had his own reasons as well...But still, he had respected her will when she had been struggling alone and no one else would believe in her.

Once again, she felt a hot, throbbing glow deep in her chest.

"But is it really okay to let Bell Cranell go on his own?" Ouka asked, clearly concerned.

"You're right that it will be difficult, but the fact that Mr. Bell will be able to maneuver much more easily on his own far outweighs the risk. I think this is the best way for him to get ahead of the other adventurers and make contact with Miss Lyu," Lilly answered.

Plus, she pointed out, the rest of the party members would have a hard time making their way even through this floor alone, whereas Bell could get around as a solo player even in the lower levels.

"Anyway, Welf has just finished making him some extra-tough protective gear," she said, glancing at the smith.

"Bell, take this."

"Welf...what is this?"

"It's a Goliath Scarf. I made it from a piece of Li'l E's robe."

Bell stared at the jet-black cloth that Welf was holding out. It was a section of the Goliath Robe, which offered a protective power equal to an iron wall. Although it wouldn't cover as much area as the robe, the giant's defensive gear was as strong and durable as anything available.

"I made it on the sly while you guys were fighting on the twenty-first floor. It wasn't easy; believe me! I didn't have a proper setup, so I had to use a magic blade to cut it off."

"Uh, Welf...are you sure it's okay?" Bell asked, looking up at his friend.

As Bell well knew, the smith was reluctant to let his contracted partner use an unimproved drop item from a monster. But despite his craftsman's pride, Welf nodded.

"Yeah. To be honest, I'd prefer you to get by with only the armor I've made for you...But if something was to happen to you, I'd never forgive myself. After all, I said I'd stop weighing my pride against our friendship, didn't I?"

He smiled as he handed Bell the Goliath Scarf.

"Sorry, man—it's not very stylish."

"No worries. But I bet this thing will give me a sore neck!" Bell joked, wrapping the scarf around his neck. The price of the drop item's incredible defensive power was its equally incredible weight.

As the two laughed and joked like brothers, Welf seemed to suddenly remember something, and he leaned over to whisper in Bell's ear.

"When I was making this, our prophetic Mirabilis helped me out. Actually, she was the one who suggested I make it."

"Really?"

Bell stopped moving at the mention of Cassandra's nickname and looked in her direction. Her cheeks grew hot and she dropped her eyes.

"Um...Thank you, Miss Cassandra."

"..."

As Lilly and the others watched, Cassandra looked up at Bell, who had walked over to her. She was happy that he had thanked her and happy to see the boyish smile on his face.

Suddenly, a thought occurred to her.

Even though her prophecy had made no direct reference to Bell's death, was it okay for him to go all alone? If she let him go, something bad was sure to happen to him. She just knew it.

She'd gotten this far. Couldn't she ask for a little more?

...No, it's impossible. There's no way I can stop him.

As she looked into Bell's eyes, she gave up on the fleeting hope that had crossed her mind. No matter how much she pleaded, she knew she could not stop him. After all, hadn't she just the other day realized that a firm will was synonymous with a strong destiny?

Even if he believes in my dream, would he...?

She had wondered many times if she should tell Bell the whole truth about her prophecy, since he was the only one who believed her. But every time, she had held back.

Assuming he believed everything she told him, what would he do when he realized that such a cruel fate awaited Lyu? She knew the answer without even thinking about it. He would fly to her, knowing he was rushing toward the jaws of death.

If that was the case, she concluded it would be better not to tell him.

She herself did not understand everything. She didn't want to cloud his judgment by sharing her nonsensical dream with him.

"...Mr. Bell."

Cassandra felt that her prophetic dreams were a curse.

No one believed her.

No one took her seriously.

She didn't know if even the deities realized what was coming.

But one person...this boy...believed in her. His trust had saved her.

She didn't want to let him go. She didn't want to leave him. She didn't want to lose him.

If it meant being able to keep him by her side, she would even become his lover. His partner for life.

But this calculating emotion, more desire to be saved than true yearning for him, was warped. Even if she felt suddenly attracted to him, it wasn't the boy himself she was drawn to but simply the illusion that he was the only one who believed in her dreams. That was all she thought it was, at least.

Therefore, she was definitely not the right woman for him.

But she wanted him to live...at the very least. It was okay to want that, wasn't it?

"Please come back alive," she said, her voice full of emotion. If the others had heard her, she knew they would think she was being overly dramatic.

"When we're back on the surface together...there are many things I'd like to...tell you," she added.

All she could do was entrust everything to this boy.

To the white light whose end she had not been able to foresee even in her dream.

As the prophetess looked up at him with wavering eyes, Bell smiled brightly, as if to sweep away tragedy.

"Yes, I promise. I'll come back."

CHAPTER 3
THE TRUE INTENTIONS OF GALE WIND

Flames of rage.

That was the only way to describe the impulse that seared her heart.

The feeling that overtook her when she saw him from behind.

The instant she glimpsed his profile.

The moment her eyes met his.

The emotion in the depths of her heart surged upward.

He's alive!

He's alive!

He's alive!

It's him—that man!

Who could snuff out the flames of rage that flared within her the moment she realized?

The hand that gripped her wooden sword shook, and the weapon itself let out an indistinct cry of rage.

That was the spark. She shrugged off the cloak of justice and became no more than a beast chasing after the group of men as they screamed in terror.

She did not know how many times silver flashed.

She could not remember how much blood spurted into the air.

She was spurred by righteous indignation from the instant she realized.

No, righteous indignation was just a front. In truth, she may simply have wanted to hurl her wildly raging emotions against them. Already, she had lost sight of which was her true self.

All she knew was that she was being driven forward. Driven by the flames of rage. By the black emotions.

She told herself, conveniently, that it was "a sense of mission."

This time. This time I will be sure.

Her blade was ravenous, and her heart was raging.

Her memories of the past screamed for her to settle things, once and for all.

As she sped through the Dungeon as quick as the wind, a thought occurred to her.

Her first friend seemed to have said something to her hotheaded self.

Her second friend seemed to have forgiven her despite her mistakes.

Her third friend, the boy...What would he think if he saw her now?

That was her one lingering concern as fiery resentment burned fiercely in the back of her mind and the pit of her stomach.

And there was something else.

She pretended not to notice that her hand, the hand that had gripped theirs, was throbbing as if weeping.

Only the most skilled adventurers in the hunting party and those with a certain amount of experience in the Water Capital have been selected to continue on to the twenty-seventh floor.

I am joining this elite group led by Bors as a representative of *Hestia Familia*. At first, he looked upset that I was the only member of our group to volunteer, but when I explained about needing to move quickly—and after Aisha gave him a few threatening words—he agreed.

I head out of the twenty-fifth floor, the Goliath Scarf from Welf and Cassandra wrapped around my neck and the parting words of Lilly and the others at my back.

"UOOOOOOOOOO!"

Atrocious roars echo through misty air.

Monsters rush toward us, their yellow eyes flashing.

Mermen.

The half-fish, half-human monsters are covered in blue scales. Like humans, they walk on two feet, and their hands with fins running down the backs skillfully handle landforms, the nature weapons of the Dungeon. With scales covering their whole body, the monsters remind me of an underwater version of lizardmen. They're among the stronger opponents we're likely to encounter on the twenty-sixth floor.

The half-fish warriors scramble out of the stream that runs through the passageway and climb onto land one after the next, gripping crystal maces, a type of lower-level nature weapon.

"Errrgh!"

I leap aside to avoid a mace that smashes into the crystal floor and bring down Hakugen above the merman's head.

The blindingly quick blow I release as I twist my hips away easily slices through its neck.

The featherlight, glittering knife continues in a perfect curve, like it's swimming through the air, and knocks down the other crystal maces on their way toward my body.

"?!"

I dive into the center of the horde, and the mermen flinch at my acrobatic battle moves. I take advantage of their momentary weakness to place a hand on the ground and let loose a spinning kick that all but skims the ground.

The kick lands powerfully on the legs of several mermen, causing them to stumble to the ground, tangled together.

"Bors!"

"Yeah!"

An instant later, Bors and the other adventurers are beating their weapons against the collapsed mermen. The rain of greatswords and hammers literally beats them to a pulp.

Essentially, the battle strategy of the mermen is to move in groups. But once their leader is killed, the group falls into chaos!

This is my first encounter with mermen, but thanks to Eina's lessons, I already know about their habits and attack methods. I'm putting into practice the textbook methods for taking them down, but I also add in my own lightning-quick attacks.

My eyes zero in on the leader, who is being protected by other mermen, as he lets out a series of hideous screeches. I head straight for him.

Is the Goliath Scarf slowing me down? Maybe, but not too much!

The item is the polar opposite of Hakugen, and I can sense it pressing down on my body as I kick into gear.

Ignoring the reactions of the monsters surrounding me, I head for the gaping merman leader, drawing the black knife from my waist as I move.

"Yah!!"

"Gya?!"

The Divine Knife that I've slipped from its sheath rips through the leader's body. The fierce blow lands like a spear piercing his chest, and the mermen's kingpin disintegrates instantly into ash.

"Shit, it's a light quartz!"

"!"

A second later, I'm whipping my head around in response to Bors's yell from behind me.

Several purple crystal forms about the size and shape of bucklers are floating in the passageway, which is around five meders tall. In the center of each one is a single pale-yellow organ that appears to be an eye.

Light quartzes are inorganic monsters that float about adventurers' heads, and as their crystalline outer appearance would suggest, they have no means of engaging in close combat. Instead, their single but extremely menacing means of attack is to shoot out beams of light!

"!"

"Ack!"

We leap back in unison as a light quartz shoots a narrow beam. The amber ray of light burns a line into the Dungeon's crystal floor and walls as it passes over them. Bors and the others scramble for shelter. Then they wait for their chance.

The typical way to defeat a light quartz is to get it to emit all its power, then attack it while it's recharging. And indeed, no approach could be more correct.

But me—I fly right into the gushing beams of light.

I figure the golden beams are never going to end.

"Hey, Rabbit Foot?!"

As the confused voices of the upper-class adventurers beat at my back, I speed up.

My enemy is floating in midair.

It's too far to reach with my knife.

A Firebolt might work…

I think I'll try something else first.

Obeying the voice in the back of my mind, which is almost like a flash of inspiration, I put my right hand on the scarf around my neck.

The next instant, I've ripped it off and am swinging it through the air like a weapon.

It's sure heavy enough!

I'm wielding it like a whip, or rather a chain.

It blocks and repels the beams from multiple light quartzes before crashing straight into them!

"—?!"

The black scarf accelerates like a whirlwind, smashing some crystal forms to smithereens and sending others crashing to the floor.

The crushed light quartzes either go silent as the light disappears from their eyes or lose their magic stones and turn to ash.

"Yesss…!"

This protective gear fashioned from the Goliath Robe is really something. It's so tough it can defend against anything, be it blade or flames, but on the flip side, it can also be turned into the toughest of weapons. I silently cheer the scarf for the excellent job it did in repelling every single one of the light-quartz rays.

"Ouch..."

I rub my right arm as I continue to grin excitedly. The unaccustomed movements and weight of the scarf may have injured my tendons. As I rub a generous amount of potion onto my arm, I tell myself it might be best not to use this particular weapon too much until I'm used to it.

In contrast to the Firebolt, which is a long-distance weapon that moves in a straight line, the scarf is a midrange, indirect weapon. It just might help me add variety to my attack methods. I feel slightly bad about using the item Welf made as a protector in this way, but...

"Hey, Rabbit Foot...is this really your first time on this floor?" Bors asks, walking up to me.

Since I've killed all the monsters, the other adventurers are putting down their weapons and squinting at me like the sun is in their eyes.

"What can I say...? You've gotten stronger. I'm gonna move you up to the front guard. I'm sure you'll do a great job!"

"Bors..."

"Go get 'em! I'll leave all the tough work to you. Oh, and we divide rare drop items fifty-fifty."

"Uh, sure," I answer, breaking into a sweat. The sincere, fatherly look on Bors's face has been replaced by a sleazy smile, like he's just stumbled upon a lucrative windfall.

Around us, the other adventurers are cleaning up from the battle. In order to prevent the emergence of enhanced species and other Irregulars, the supporters hastily collect magic stones. I look around at their faces.

There's a wicked-looking elf with a double sword, an ax-wielding animal person with a piece of cloth covering his mouth, and a dwarf with a massive shield and battle hammer.

They demonstrated plenty of battle prowess on our way through the middle levels...But even if their Statuses are higher than that of Welf and the rest of our party, they definitely aren't working in sync with one another.

That's one reason I risked making the call to take on the monsters myself. In such a quickly formed party, the shifts between offense and defense, fast and slow don't play out how I'd expect. Sometimes we're even holding one another back.

Once again, I realize just how skilled and valuable Lilly, Welf, and the other members of our party are in the way they adjust to support me.

Plus, the monsters here...they're just different from the ones in the middle levels.

The long-distance light-quartz attacks were a bother, and totally different from the flames that hellhounds release...But more importantly, the monsters down here, like the merman leader, are *really intelligent*. Way more so than in the upper and middle levels.

They may not be very good at it, but the fact that monsters here can coordinate their actions at all makes them an immeasurable menace.

I absolutely can't let myself get overly confident.

"Okay, I'm gonna split up the party again! We're too inefficient when we move as a single group! If anyone finds Gale Wind, try to drive her into the cavern! Worst-case scenario, we confirm she's here and pull back to the twenty-fifth floor! If we take up positions there, Aisha will have to come help us at some point!"

Bors shouts these commands as we pass through the tunnel connecting the twenty-sixth and twenty-seventh floors, bypassing the plunge pool on the twenty-sixth floor, which forms the middle step in the three floors connected by the Great Falls.

We've charged down to the twenty-seventh floor all at once, and now it looks like we'll be splitting up to search for Gale Wind...that is, Lyu.

"You, Rabbit Foot! Come with me!"

"Uh, um, okay."

Bors makes the executive decision to take me, a Level 4 adventurer, along with him. The other adventurers boo and jeer disapprovingly.

Is he using me as a kind of all-rounder?

In any case, our group of five turns off onto a side passage. It's one of several main routes leading to the passage that connects to the twenty-eighth floor. This part of the Dungeon is comprised of faintly striped deep-blue crystals. A wide waterway flows directly next to the dryland path. It's flowing way faster than the rivers on the floors above us. A dim light emanates from clusters of white crystal, illuminating the darkness.

Everywhere we go, I see the remains of old passageways that have collapsed in on themselves, and piles of crystals that appear to be the result of cave-ins block our way. This must be the aftermath of the explosions we heard earlier.

I'm leading our group, but all of us are constantly on the lookout for monsters. We press forward as the path leads down countless stairways and slopes winding through the multilayered floor.

"Hey, Bell Cranell. Do you remember when we fought the Goliath?"

"Yeah, we charged that whopper with you."

"You can count on us, Rabbit Foot!"

"Uh, yeah. That's great!"

The skilled upper-class adventurers in our group are bantering back and forth to keep us all from getting too tense.

There are a pair of cheerful animal-person siblings and a masculine Amazonian warrior. I really admire their friendliness.

Probably thanks to the battle with the Black Goliath, residents of Rivira have tended to treat me amiably. The other upper-class adventurers often ask me about my epic clash with the minotaur Asterios in Orario and generally seem to admire me.

It's a huge honor to be accepted in this way by the senior adventurers, and I can't help smiling to myself about it...But I also feel bad that I'm going to have to slip away from this group in the near future.

I need to do it, though, for Lyu's sake.

I think it will be easier for me to move around if I look for a chance to break off from them...But I won't find her by searching at random...

The long series of explosions we heard on our way here has fallen silent now.

The roar of the distant Great Falls echoes even here, drowning out softer noises that might give away her location. Finding Lyu alone on this immense floor is going to be extremely difficult.

Still…it's not like I don't have a goal.

I convinced Aisha and the others to let me go alone, and it would be wrong to say I have no strategy whatsoever. I'm leaving it all up to manpower…or monsterpower?

I'm busy thinking about how I can get them to find her when—

"B-B-Bors?!"

One of the animal people, who has been peering into a passageway that branches off our current route to the right, shouts out.

He sounds terrified, like something unusual is going on. We rush to his side.

"What…?"

I lose all words when I see it.

"What in the world is this?"

Bors and the rest of us look up.

We see a hole.

A huge vertical hole leading to the floor above us.

It's not a tidy hole like those in the Stone Cavern Maze. Instead, it looks like *something* has forcefully dug its way through the ceiling.

A stream is trickling noisily down like a miniature waterfall.

"…I've never seen a huge hole like this on the twenty-seventh floor…" Bors groans in a low voice.

Something unusual is happening in the Dungeon—something even these upper-class adventurers who have passed through the Water Capital many times have never seen before.

In a corner of my mind, an alarm bell starts to chime softly.

"I don't mind staying back…but it sure as hell looks like we'll be camped out here for a while."

Welf rubbed his throat as if to thaw it.

He was standing on a cliff at the far southern end of the twenty-fifth floor. The space was about the size of a small "room," big enough to fit several dozen adventurers. In fact, it was the exact spot where Lilly had suggested setting up a base when she and the others had been separated from Bell by the moss huge, and indeed, it was plenty large enough for that purpose. It was also a perfect location for fending off attacks by winged monsters.

Several hours had passed since the hunting party, including Bell, set off in pursuit of Gale Wind. Now, the adventurers who had stayed behind were each absorbed in their own tasks.

Which is to say, they were either arguing over who would be on guard duty or relaxing.

"They don't have much fighting spirit, do they? Of course, I suppose that's to be expected."

"Well, it would be hard to find something to do right now. You wouldn't want to go off hunting monsters to kill time and then be too tired to help at the critical moment."

Mikoto and Ouka were chatting as they watched the other adventurers. Those remaining on the twenty-fifth floor represented the group Bors had not selected for his elite hunting party, and some were sulking over their exclusion. These individuals did not think they were Gale Wind's equal in battle, but they had hoped to somehow steal a portion of the spoils. It wasn't hard to guess how they felt about being made to wait for the prize that had been dangled before their eyes. Most didn't know what to do with themselves in the meantime.

For Lilly, Mikoto, Chigusa, and Daphne—who weren't yet accustomed to the Water Capital—just gazing out from the cliffs at the magnificent Great Falls was enough to keep them from getting bored.

"..."

Normally, Cassandra would have felt the same, but now, tormented by her prophetic dream, all she could do was pray desperately for the future and for Bell's safe return. And so she stood by the edge of the sheer cliff, gazing out at the Great Falls that continued on to the twenty-seventh floor.

"...Nothing suspicious so far, it seems," said Welf, who was sitting down.

"You'd better not be too obvious about it; he might notice you," Lilly warned casually as she distributed travel rations.

Welf had been watching the werewolf who Bell was concerned about.

"His name is Turk Sledd. I asked around a bit, and it seems he's been living in Rivira for about three years," she said.

"What's his Status?"

"Assuming he hasn't made any false reports, he's a Level Two. He hangs around second-tier adventurers, but I hear he's been down to the lower levels himself a bunch of times," Lilly said unhesitatingly in response to the question from Welf, who along with the others was tearing off pieces of the salted meat with his hands to eat.

The residents of Rivira seemed to place a certain degree of trust in Turk, she added.

The others didn't know quite what to make of this information. Suddenly, Aisha—who had been lying down with her eyes closed—jerked up.

"I've rested enough...Should I attack?"

"What are you talking about?"

The whole group was staring at Aisha, whose words seemed completely nonsensical.

"We're just wasting time sitting around being suspicious of people. Don't you think the fastest solution is for me to beat him to a pulp?"

Ouka and the others grimaced uncomfortably at the unreasonably aggressive words of the Level 4 Amazon, who was clearly the strongest adventurer present.

"Whew, that's a real Amazonian way of thinking...But if he's actually hiding something, I doubt you'll be able to torture the information out of him. And you'll probably turn his buddies against us, too," Daphne said in a bored tone.

"All right, I don't have a choice…The rest of you keep a watch."

"Wh-wh-what are you planning to do?" Mikoto asked tensely, once again having a bad feeling about Aisha's intentions.

"It's obvious, isn't it? I'm gonna pull him into that cave and devour him. His lips will be looser after I've straddled him and made him howl—"

"Aiii! Aiii! Aiii!"

Tossing aside her manners, Haruhime—who was blushing to the tips of her ears—let out a series of shrieks and flapped her hands in frantic denial of Aisha's suggestion. Aisha clicked her tongue in dissatisfaction.

Not only Mikoto, Chigusa, and Cassandra but even Lilly and Daphne were blushing. The two lone males, Welf and Ouka, looked extremely uncomfortable. The other adventurers standing around nearby shot the mixed-faction party dirty looks for making such a ruckus.

"This is not *Ishtar Familia*!" Haruhime said, covering her red face with both hands and looking almost on the verge of tears.

"—Okay, let's get going!"

Just then, the subject of their argument shifted into action.

"I can't stand leaving everything in Bors's hands! For the sake of my murdered friend, Jan, I'm going to slaughter Gale Wind!"

"If we get carried away, we'll probably end up being beaten by our intended victim. Anyway, didn't Bors tell us to guard this area?"

"We're still adventurers! Don't you at least have the guts to kill the fugitive and make a name for yourself?"

"…I'm going with Turk. Sitting around here twiddling our thumbs is a joke."

Reactions to the werewolf's call to action were split: Some opposed him, while others sided with him.

The latter group was far smaller than the former.

"We don't want to make Bors mad. But if you want to go, then go."

"I'll go and show you all how it's done!"

In the end, a group of four set off for the twenty-seventh floor. Although Bors's supporters quarreled with the departing group, they did not stop them from leaving, and so Turk and those who had taken his side headed down the path that led west along the cliff's edge.

"Let's go," Lilly said, standing. Welf and the others nodded silently in response to her brief words.

Cassandra alone was filled with worry. She could not let them go off without her, however, so she, too, followed the group into the maze of the twenty-fifth floor.

We can't take our eyes off the huge hole. Water is falling from it in a thin stream and pooling on the floor.

As we stand here still as statues looking upward, I notice something.

"It's beginning to repair itself," I whisper.

The Dungeon is starting to reestablish its composition. The process is so subtle you wouldn't notice unless you stood here staring at it, but gradually, the crystal ceiling is filling back in, and the hole is closing.

Judging by the state of things, the repair has just begun. That means the hole was probably made recently.

In other words, whatever made the hole is…

"…It's still nearby, isn't it?"

At Bors's words, the temperature in the passageway seems to drop. At the same time, our group takes up defensive positions. We scan the surroundings and grip our weapons tensely.

It's possible that some unknown Irregular with the ability to gouge through the stone walls of the Dungeon is on this floor. My eardrums throb with the sound of rushing water that echoes through the passageways.

Something cold drips onto my back.

"…This isn't the work of Gale Wind, is it…?"

"I doubt she could do this even with magic…It seems like something dug down from the top, rather than blasting through."

Speculation flies back and forth among the adventurers, who have finally let down their guard after several uneventful hours. I realize that the whole party is disturbed.

There's an iron rule among adventurers: If something unusual happens in the Dungeon, run.

Bors is struggling to make a decision, a deep wrinkle etched between his brows. Should we continue on toward our goal or flee this floor?

All of us sense that this isn't an Irregular we'll be able to ignore.

...Why now...?

I don't know why, but suddenly I think of Cassandra's face, worrying and worrying about something.

"What do we do, Bors?"

"Normally I'd haul ass out of here...but we can't forget about the rest of the adventurers we split off from. Whether or not we keep chasing Gale Wind, I want to tell them about this."

I feel increasingly distressed as I listen to their conversation. There's a good chance Lyu is on this floor. If some sort of Irregular is creeping around here, she'll be at risk, too. I'm just thinking that I need to find her as quickly as possible when—

"...?"

Are we being...watched?

I've gotten very sensitive to the feeling of other people (or things) looking at me, and I sense eyes on me right now. But it's not an unpleasant feeling...I don't know quite how to put it...but could it be someone I know?

I look up in surprise. Just then—

"Hey, did you hear that...?!"

"What's that song?...Is Gale Wind singing? No, it's..."

"...'The Song that Echoes in the Dungeon.'"

The animal-person siblings and the Amazon forget everything as they listen to the beautiful melody. Bors, too, stands agape and murmurs the name of a song that adventurers whisper about among themselves.

I dash away from them as if I've been hurled forward.

"H-hey, Rabbit Foot?!"

"I'll go check it out!"

The voices of my companions trying to stop me are already far in the distance.

I can sense them chasing after me in a flurry, and I run even faster. I feel bad, but in order to ditch Bors and the others, I race randomly through the passageways.

Whenever I encounter a monster, I try to get around it. If I can't avoid it, I put on a show with my knife, and when the monster shrinks back in fear, I rush past it. Sometimes I avoid a fight by leaping right over their heads.

The song is moving!

Whoever is singing is watching my actions and moving toward a place where we can meet.

The voice drifts in and out, but it's always beautiful. The quiet song is like the seashore on a moonlit night, leading me forward. Finally, I arrive in a large room with a spring in it.

In the center of the spring, sitting on a crystal rock and continuing to sing, is a stunningly beautiful mermaid.

"Mari!"

I call out the Xenos mermaid's name. The last time I saw her was the day I fought the moss huge. It's hard to believe that was only two days ago.

She looks just as I remember, her long emerald-blue hair adorned with ornaments made of shells and pearls. She's put on a bikini top made of shells out of consideration for me, which is a relief. We first met on the twenty-fifth floor, but I suspect she can move freely anywhere within the Water Capital.

It feels strange to meet again so soon, but I step into the spring up to my waist and walk toward her. She turns to face me and pushes off the crystal rocks with both hands.

Then she hugs me fiercely.

"Bell!"

She throws herself at my chest like a child and wraps her arms around me. I start to blush at the soft sensation of her body, but then I notice something.

"Mari…?"

She's shaking…

I can feel her fear, and it surprises me. I put my hands on her shoulders.

"What's wrong, Mari? Did something happen?"

"…"

I speak in a gentle voice to calm her.

Although I had wanted to call on her to help me find Lyu, she was the one who called out to me. Why? She was even willing to risk being discovered by Bors and the rest of our group.

She looks down for a moment, then moves her petite lips.

"Something is here…that shouldn't be here…"

Something that shouldn't be here…?

Right away, I think of the huge hole we discovered just a short while ago.

Is whatever made that hole lurking around the twenty-seventh floor?

"Mari, do you know something? What did you see?"

"I don't know…I don't know when it came, and I don't know where it went…I never saw it before…!"

Mari's speech and actions make her seem younger than Wiene, and she speaks human poorly. I can tell that she herself is frustrated by her inability to describe what she saw.

But what she says is enough.

Something that scared Mari this much is on this floor. I squeeze her shoulders and ask another question.

"Mari, I'm looking for someone. Have you seen an elf girl?"

"Elf…?"

"Um, her ears are longer than mine, and she has a wooden sword, and she's definitely hiding her face…and she's really fast."

I tell her all the concrete details I can think of.

"I really, really want to meet with her," I add.

Mari looks up at me for a few moments. Then she nods.

But the next minute, she's burying her head in my chest and rubbing it back and forth, as if to say she doesn't want to tell me because it's dangerous.

"...Wait."

She moves away from me slightly, closes her eyes, and begins to sing again.

This time, it's not an enchanting melody but a discordant one: her own special song to charm not humans but fellow monsters. Mari has the ability to control monsters with lower abilities than hers.

As waves ripple out from where she sits in the water, howls echo back to her from various directions. She opens her eyes wide as she listens to the voices of the monsters giving her information about the missing elf.

"I know now, Bell...She's over there!"

"Thank you!"

As Mari dives into the spring and starts to swim, I climb onto land and begin running.

Just like before, I move through the water-and-crystal-filled maze guided by the mermaid.

What will I do when I meet up with Lyu? Should I ask her about what happened on the eighteenth floor? But can I really take the time to do that with irregularities occurring on the floor? Bors and the other adventurers are at risk...!

All sorts of worries and questions are flying around inside my head. Thinking about everything I need to do is driving me crazy.

Just then, a powerful shock thunders through the floor.

"An explosion?! Again?!" I shout as the reverberations rock through me.

The explosions had stopped for a while, but now they've started again.

Mari, who's in the water, flinches at the sound. Waves rise in the stream she is swimming down—evidence of the explosion's strength.

The sound and shaking seem to be coming from nearby!

I run faster, guided by reverberations and sounds that seem to be coming from collapsing crystals.

Mari is leading me in the same direction, and I follow her tail fin as it cuts through the water.

An ominous feeling runs down my neck.

I desperately try to ignore it.

Turning a corner littered with fragments of crystal, I realize we've reached the source of the shaking.

"Oh no...!"

Everything is a big mess. The ground has burst open and is totally unrecognizable, while the crystal walls have avalanched into the river alongside the path, blocking its flow. Water has started to gush from the cracks in the ceiling, pouring down in a waterfall. The destruction etched into the crystal maze looks like the aftermath of a barrage of explosions.

Smoke is drifting through the air, as if some kind of item or magic was used, and beyond the smoke is...a humanoid figure.

Mari, who's come with me this far, dives in a panic to the bottom of the water.

My body stiff, I stare ahead of me for several seconds.

The smoke wavers and begins to clear—

"—"

Words fail me as the scene comes into focus.

A dwarf lies collapsed on the ground. He's on his back, convulsing and bleeding.

And there, *standing with one foot on the dwarf's shoulder*, is a woman.

The very woman who has come to our rescue so many times is standing with her back to me, the hem of her long mantle-like cape flapping.

She's thrust her wooden sword into the ground right next to the dwarf's face. In the other hand, she holds up a bloody shortsword.

I glimpse her sky-blue eyes beneath the hood pulled up over her head. They are wide open, and they make my blood run cold.

My heart quivers at the sight of her profile, which reveals her emotions so nakedly.

"Miss…Lyu…?"

I call her name, half in doubt. I have seen this expression on her face only once before.

Her ears twitch.

Time stops as she turns and pierces me with her sky-blue eyes. As astonishment spreads over her face, I know. It's Lyu.

Before my eyes is the unmistakable, beautiful elf I know so well.

"Miss Ly—"

"Why are you here?!"

I stop breathing as she scolds me fiercely.

I've never heard her speak in such an angry voice.

I've never seen her glare like this.

It's the expression of…a bloodthirsty murderer.

"Why. Are. You. Here?"

A moment later, her face crumples with a range of different emotions.

What is spilling from her blurred eyes? Suffering? Sorrow?

Or regret?

"Mr. Cranell, leave this floor. Immediately."

She speaks in a low voice, her tone devoid of emotion.

My hand shakes as if an electric current is running through it, while the rest of my body remains frozen.

"You must not be here. Leave now."

"M-M-Miss Lyu, what do you mean—?"

"Just do as I say!!"

She's screaming at me again.

Her words are not a request but a demand that leaves no room for questions, let alone opposition. Meanwhile, she continues to pierce me with her sharp gaze as I stand frozen.

"You don't need to do anything. Or know anything. Don't get involved."

She says each sentence in rapid succession, then pulls her sword from the ground, takes something from the fallen dwarf, and makes a move to leave.

"Miss Lyu…Please wait, Miss Lyu! What is going on? What are you doing?!"

Time begins to slide forward again. I've finally managed to move my frozen lips and get out a few words.

I feel all turned around, and I have no idea what to say to her, but nevertheless I keep talking.

"What in the world happened to that dwarf…?!"

Lyu looks irritated by my shaking voice and glances down at the body.

"For all I care, this bastard can serve as food for the monsters."

She spits out the statement and then takes off running, leaving the battered dwarf behind.

The voice that spoke her parting words was full of hatred. I'm so shocked I can't move. I'm left behind, completely useless.

"Miss…Lyu…"

I want to know what your true intentions are.

But that question did not reach you. Far from it—instead, you rejected me and fled.

I cannot begin to understand what I just saw.

My mind isn't even churning—it's just blank. It's useless.

I'm standing here in a daze.

"Bell…Bell!"

Mari's voice brings me back to myself.

I must have been standing here for quite a few seconds, or rather minutes.

The sound of running water fills my ears again, and color returns to the scene before my eyes.

"…!"

With my mind as confused as ever, I kick the ground. After wavering for a moment over whether to chase after Lyu or stay with the dwarf, I decide on the latter and crouch next to him.

"Oh boy..."

The collapsed dwarf adventurer has already lost consciousness. His protective gear is half-destroyed, and his short trunk is covered in blood. He's marred by long, thin gashes, as if he has been slashed repeatedly.

"...!"

I can't just leave him here, so I start to treat his wounds. Every now and then he twitches, as if his body is recalling the violence inflicted on it.

All through this, though, the only thing I can think of is Lyu.

The image of her back turned to me in rejection won't leave my mind. My hands are shaking so badly, I can't properly administer first aid.

I'm more in shock than I realized.

"Miss Lyu...!"

I finish up the urgent-care measures that can't be put off, then I tuck the dwarf under one arm and start running. As the dwarf's limp arms and legs swing back and forth, I head in the direction that Lyu disappeared to, leaping over chunks of crystal that have fallen from the walls and ceilings. Mari hurries to follow behind me, dipping down to the river bottom and then popping her face above the water's surface.

"Huff, puff..."

Sweat flies backward off my body as I run at top speed, still thinking about what just happened.

I arrived on the scene just moments after the explosion happened. Lyu's magic is definitely powerful enough to cause this much damage to the passageways. Thinking back on the situation, I believe the string of events fits together.

A violent assault using magic?

A bombardment that was impossible to defend against?

Did Lyu attack this dwarf with the clear intent to kill him?

It's a lie; it can't be...Not her...!

I want to believe Lyu is not the kind of elf who would do something like that.

But what do I make of the dwarf under my arm, breathing so faintly I can barely feel it?

Did she just happen to pass by after he was attacked by a monster? And I happened to be unfortunate enough to find them both a moment later? It's such a ridiculous idea that I feel like crying.

The dwarf's deep cuts look very much like those on the corpse in Rivira.

It seems nearly incontrovertible that she inflicted these wounds on the dwarf.

Why did she attack him? What in the world could make her do this?

I don't know. I don't know anything.

My unsettled mind is unable even to piece together a theory to console myself.

I thought the incident in Rivira was some sort of mistake.

I still don't know the truth of it. But…

The look on Lyu's face, the feeling in her heart…that murderous intent…Were they real?

I shiver as I recall the expression on her face as she stood there with her wooden sword thrust into the ground, looking down on the dwarf with terrifyingly cold eyes.

Even if someone else's schemes are involved—even if she's been pulled into something—if Lyu's feelings, her intent to kill, are genuine…

If the motive driving her forward is real, then—

"!"

I shake my hair back to stop the thought in its tracks.

I'm being tormented by these speculations that appear and disappear in the back of my mind, by this illusion that I'm being strangled by my own hands.

If I don't get a handle on myself, I'll drown in my own thoughts.

As if the Dungeon is jeering at my inner conflict, another explosion thunders in the distance.

"…?!"

I change direction and head toward the explosion.

The roars of monsters mingle with shock waves. And was that a human scream I heard very faintly just now?

I have a bad feeling about this. The uneasiness won't go away. I want to tear out my heart as it beats so harshly and noisily. I readjust the dwarf under my arm and rush toward the echoing explosions.

Mari struggles to keep up with my anxious steps as she swims along the waterway beside the path.

"Mari, you can't come with me!"

"I want to come!"

Mari shakes her head like an unreasonable child in response to my warning.

I'm painfully aware of how concerned she is for me because of my strange behavior. But her concern is a problem right now. I can't drag her into a dangerous situation.

I frown, then sadly make up my mind to change course, heading toward a passageway where the dryland path continues but the waterway dead-ends.

"Oh!"

Mari gasps in surprise. Her jewellike jade eyes pool with tears.

"Dumb Bell!"

Her words fly at my back as I continue to run forward, whispering my apologies to her. I'm encountering so many monsters, it almost feels like they've caught wind of the explosion and are heading for it themselves. Devil mosquitoes, blue crabs, and even large-category crystal turtles block the road.

Aside from the winged harpies and sirens, the aquatic monsters of the Water Capital are scarcely impacted by fire-type magic. I limit my use of Firebolt to keeping them in check, but while my left hand is closed in a fist, my right hand grips Hakugen and slices through the enemies in my way.

Having dodged the monsters bearing down on me, I arrive at my destination…and see the same scene I came across a little while earlier.

"…!!"

A wall has been deeply gouged out, and crystals are raining down from the cracked ceiling.

The only difference from the earlier scene is that a large number of adventurers are screaming and shouting.

"What is going on?!"

"Everything is totally destroyed...What could have done this?!"

The site of the explosion is hellish.

The various hunting parties that split up on the twenty-seventh floor have followed the sound of the explosion and gathered here. They are clustered around an adventurer lying on the broad main route, which is scattered with crystal chunks of varying sizes.

"Eh...? He's been killed."

"But I don't recognize him from our hunting party!"

Sharp claws grip my heart at the word *killed*.

The victim is either a human or an animal person, covered in blood and severely burned all over his body. His charred eyes will see no more. The smell of burned flesh invades my nostrils, and a wave of nausea overtakes me.

My hands and feet are cold.

My chaotic emotions are making my brain go haywire.

I reel backward in shock.

I feel like I'm being baptized by the lower levels. This is different from the middle and upper levels—to have this many encounters with death.

Incoherent thoughts are born and die as I try to escape from the reality confronting me.

"...?!"

A victim here as well?

Was this, too...the work of Lyu?!

The dwarf under my arms seems to have grown heavier. Suddenly I notice that my body is covered in sweat.

"Rabbit Foot! Where the hell did you go off to?!"

"...Bors!"

As angry howls fly back and forth in the Dungeon, a voice even louder than the others calls out to me. I put the dwarf down and turn to Bors and the rest of our group, who have walked up to me.

"I'm sorry for going off on my own. But what is going on...?!"

"...We just got here, too, so we don't know, either. But it's obviously not the work of a monster. The only one who would go and do something like this..."

At this point, Bors notices the dwarf lying on the ground covered in wounds from some sort of blade.

"Hey, what's with the dwarf?"

"Th-th-this guy—"

"Don't tell me Gale Wind got to him...?!"

"Uh..."

I can't confirm or deny Bors's guess.

I find that I'm unable to stand up for her this time.

But what should I have said? *"Lyu inflicted all these wounds, but she's not a bad person"* probably wouldn't go over very well.

All I can do is stand by as Bors and the others snatch the injured adventurer away and begin treating him.

"It's no use; he's not opening his eyes. Is there anyone around who can tell us what happened?"

"Bors! There's a survivor over here! He's coming to!"

"!"

Bors and I both go pale at those words. We rush toward the adventurer who shouted to us. Collapsed on the ground next to a crystal wall is a catman.

"—"

I'm so shocked at the condition he's in that my stomach seems to flip upside down.

First of all, he's *missing an arm.*

Where a forearm should be protruding from the blood-soaked sleeve beneath his mangled upper arm, there's nothing.

His face is covered in burns, slashes, and blood, and as for the ears that mark him as an animal person...one is missing.

He has so many wounds I want to turn my eyes away.

"Hey, can you talk? What happened here?"

Bors's question is more like a shout.

The animal person has the fingers of his left hand in his mouth, dulling the chattering of his teeth. He looks up at Bors as if he's just noticed he's there. Then he curls his body—which is extremely tall and thin even for a catman—into an exaggerated cat's pose.

"G-G-Gale Wind…Leon did…"

"You say it was Gale Wind?!"

"She threw her magic at me, and I saw a flash of light, and everything went white…!"

"…!"

Bors is fixated on the second name the catman mentions, while I'm in shock over the rest of what he said.

As I stand there frozen, Bors leans forward and is about to ask where she is now when our Amazonian party member stops him.

"Wait, Bors, we should treat him first—"

The catman widens his eyes as she reaches out a hand.

"Don't touch me!"

"?!"

"Don't touch me, please…!"

He collapses farther onto the ground in an attempt to move away from her. With his one remaining hand, he clutches his head and repeatedly flinches as if in fear. It makes for such a miserable sight that Bors and the others are at a loss for what to do.

They seem to have descended into chaos…No, more like panic.

"…? Hey, aren't you…Jura Harma of *Rudra Familia*?"

As the catman rubs his disheveled hair against the floor, a vulgar ear ornament made from a monster's bone comes into view, and Bors widens his one eye as the catman's identity dawns on him.

The catman jerks in surprise, too.

"Bors, you know him?"

"Yeah…He usually goes by the name Slaver Cat. He belongs to a gang of Evils called *Rudra Familia*…The faction that entrapped and slaughtered the very same *Astrea Familia* that Gale Wind belonged to…"

My heart gives the loudest thump it's made all day.

So this is the enemy of *Astrea Familia*...of Lyu?

"Five years ago, when Gale Wind went wild, she annihilated *Rudra Familia*. Massacred all their members. At least we thought she killed them all...but it seems this one survived."

Bors ignores my dumbfounded look and glares down severely at the man he called Jura.

"Y-yeah...I was the only one who survived her attack—the attack by Leon, that piece of shit!"

The catman, who's shaking violently, doesn't deny he's an Evil.

He seems upset, but he looks at Bors and the rest of us pleadingly.

"But I haven't done anything bad since then...! Honestly, I've just been hiding out in that gloomy dungeon...!"

"...!"

"But then Leon found me, and I fled here...!"

As Bors and the rest of our group digest this surprising information, I'm the only one who seems to realize that the "dungeon" he's referring to is not this one. It's Knossos.

Just like the violent hunters of *Ikelos Familia* said, the man-made dungeon was both a breeding ground and a hideout for Evils. And this guy was hanging around down there.

But...Oh, okay...Now things are falling into place.

Even I can make a guess at what this whole thing is about.

Lyu discovered that an enemy of her former familia was alive, and as the flames of rage flared once again, she gave herself over to the desire for revenge.

And now she is pursuing him exactly as her wild emotions dictate: not with tears or blood but instead with the cold cruelty I witnessed on her face.

"Was Jan killed in Rivira because he was connected to this guy...?"

Bors and the others have their hands over their mouths, like they finally get it. I replay in my mind the scene we're all imagining.

"I'm begging you—help me...! I won't do any more evil. Hand me over to the Guild, anything, just protect me from her...!"

The catman flattens himself to the ground in prostration and entreaty. It doesn't look like a performance. No, that terror of Gale Wind and those quivering eyes and body are definitely real.

I'm stuck between the reality before my eyes and the scene playing in my mind.

I can't decide what the truth is.

I just keep asking the image of Lyu that floats in my mind, *Is it really true?*

"...You're still following us?"

"Stop it with your weird questions. We're gonna beat Gale Wind to a pulp, right? Obviously it's better to move in a group."

Aisha smirked, unembarrassed, as the werewolf Turk craned his neck around to look at her.

They were on the twenty-fifth floor.

Lilly and the others had started out following Turk's group of four, but very soon they had merged together.

Following someone undetected in the Dungeon was just about impossible. As soon as a monster discovered an adventurer, it would start howling and thrashing, which put an end to any sneaking around. It might have been slightly more possible for a solo adventurer, but Lilly and the others wanted to avoid splitting up their party, so that option had been ruled out.

The simplest option was just to join up with the group they wanted to follow. That way, if the group did anything suspicious, they could monitor them or rein in their actions.

"After all, we're hunting a Level Four adventurer," Aisha said, driving home her point.

Turk turned back toward the path ahead of him. The other adventurers in his group kept throwing suspicious glances backward and whispering.

Lilly's group was following Turk's through the Dungeon at a distance of about three meders.

"They're definitely watching us, too."

"Well, it's only natural to be irritated when another party latches on to you like this...But still, the way his temper flares up worries me."

Welf and Lilly were speaking in low voices. Meanwhile, Ouka was keeping half an eye on Turk as he watched for monster attacks. The whole group had a nervous tension about it that was different from usual.

Cassandra alone was sunk in thought.

She was thinking of Bell on the twenty-seventh floor.

I wonder if I should have told him about my dream...But if he knew the contents of the prophecy, he would definitely...

The reason she hadn't told him was that she had sensed she wouldn't have been able to alter his strong will, which was equivalent to his destiny. Plus, there was something else.

If Gale Wind is at the root of everything...

Cassandra's thoughts grew frightening.

Gale Wind—"the fairy fated to guide all to ruin"—seemed to be the prime source of the misfortune in her dream. And indeed, weren't her actions behind everything from the murder in Rivira to the "great calamity"?

If Gale Wind was the cause of all misfortune, then Bell's attempts to save her would be meaningless. Even worse—the person he had believed in would betray him, and he would face a harsh reality.

It was truly a cruel fate for the boy.

It's always the same. I worry, I waffle, I suffer, I fail...and I regret.

Anxiety and sorrow filled Cassandra's face as she stared absently at the waterway running through the Dungeon.

No one noticed her, and no one understood.

What should I have done to help him?

No answer came to her.

The adventurers around me are still in an uproar.

The assembled group winces at the smell of burned flesh. The whole passageway is in ruins, a testament to the destructive power of the violent explosion. Some monsters seem to have been caught up in the disaster as well, as evidenced by the corpse of a merman lying on the ground, its upper body crushed.

Some adventurers are hurling abuse at the monsters that wander in from other passageways, but those of us gathered around the victim are cloaked in heavy silence.

The catman called Jura is still terrified of Gale Wind. His actual age is unclear, probably due to the effects of his Status, but he looks to be in his mid-thirties. Perhaps from exhaustion, he has sunken black circles around his almond-shaped eyes, which are filled with fear.

"Bors…Wh-wh-what do we do?"

"Not much, I'd say…If we turn him in to the Guild, we'll make off with a tidy bundle of reward money and that's it. If he's killed by Gale Wind, it all disappears," Bors answers boastfully, as if proclaiming his disinterest in justice. "What are we here for? To kill the elf who murdered our fellow townsman, right? Our job hasn't changed. Just a question of whether we get more money or not."

Bors's firm stance wipes the indecision from the faces of the other adventurers. For me, though, it's a terrible decision. My face stiffens.

But I, too, am wavering.

I can't read Lyu's true intentions.

Has she really been overtaken by her desire for revenge?

Was she driven by rage to kill these adventurers?

And…

My mind is catching on something else.

I don't know what it is…but something about this situation, this course of events, makes me feel *sick to my stomach.*

In the back of my mind, a voice is shouting that something here is off.

A memory is struggling to rise to the surface of my consciousness.

…But I can't grab hold of it.

My thoughts and emotions are all mixed up. I have no idea what is true or what I should believe!

However much the deities have told me I've grown, I'm still the same old Bell Cranell.

I get confused easily and can't make decisions on my own. I'm still the same old pitiful me, constantly unsure what to do—

"—?"

As I press my hand to the side of my head to push out this feeling of despair, I stamp my boots on the ground—and hit something.

"It's a…"

Scarlet fragment.

It seems to have originated inside the Dungeon.

I pinch what appears to be a small piece of deep-red crystal between my fingers and stare at it intently. Finally, I open my eyes wide.

"It's—Gale Wind?!"

At almost the same instant, someone thunders out Lyu's name.

"?!"

I whip my head around toward source of the yell.

Far in the distance, down one of the many side passages, I glimpse something flying alongside a waterway.

It's a long cape, whipped by the wind, charging at lightning speed toward us.

"Get her, troops!!"

Bors is yelling so loud, his veins are popping out. He seems to think the critical moment has come.

I have no time to stop them. No one is about to listen to an excuse or explanation. In response to the order from their leader, who's just spit on the ground, the adventurers raise a battle cry and flood toward the lone elf.

But she doesn't even glance at them. Instead, she roars straight toward us, a bloodcurdling expression on her face.

"JURAAAAAAAAAAAAAAAAAAAAAAAAAAAAAAAAAA!!"

It's hard to believe such a massively powerful roar of anger could have come from such a delicate form.

Her cry reverberates all the way to where we stand, quite a distance from her. It shakes the Dungeon's crystal walls.

Although she might not have intended it to, the sound makes every one of the adventurers who had been racing toward her tremble with fear, as if they've just heard a monster's roar.

She keeps charging straight toward the man whose name she has screamed.

"Get out of the way!!"

"""Aaah!!"""

The scene before my eyes is unbelievable.

Gale Wind pierces the wall of upper-class adventurers—including some Level Threes—like an arrow.

Her wooden sword topples a dwarf on the front line and then, on its return blow, smashes against a wall an animal person who was flying toward her. Amazons and humans alike are trampled as they try to hold back her charge. The sword literally throws off a *blue-green glow.* It pulses along with the light of her sky-blue eyes, and each time it does, another hardened warrior is thrown into the air.

Is she going to take down all twenty upper-class adventurers…?!

"JURAAAA!"

"Aaaaaaaaaaaaaah!!"

As the masked elf glares fiercely from the depths of her hood and repeatedly screams his name, the catman goes as pale as if the world is ending. Then he turns away from her and flees.

I watch his receding form in surprise, but Bors's party is doing the opposite: Weapons raised, they're licking their chops at Gale Wind, who's broken through the wall of adventurers.

"She's using some kind of magic or skill! Stop her! If we can just slow down her momentum, we can beat her with numbers!! Don't let her take advantage of us!"

Bors is not only the head of Rivira, he also displays the confidence of a top-grade Level Three adventurer, and his commands are swift and precise. He's confident that with this many resources on our side, we can beat her. His orders fuel the fighting spirit of the animal-person siblings and the Amazon, who rush forward.

But.

"—"

The instant before they make contact, the elf's body shifts suddenly from a full-force forward charge to a whirling maelstrom.

As she spins around like a top, her cape letting out sharp popping sounds as it cuts through the wind, she slips splendidly past their outstretched arms. Then, as they stand dazed at having been played this way, she hits them on the back of the heads with her wooden sword as she completes her turn. They go flying, knocked unconscious.

Her skill is so tremendous, it takes my breath away and makes me gape in a way that's not quite appropriate for the current situation.

"What, you think you're in *Loki Familia* or something?!"

Bors, who's rapidly becoming the last man standing, flings spit and curses as he brandishes his huge battle-ax. But just before he's about to bring the blade down on this extraordinary elven warrior, who truly embodies the storm and drive that inspired her nickname—

"—? Huh? You're the same elf who...Ergh!!"

Bors pauses for an instant as if he's remembering something—most likely the battle they fought side by side on the eighteenth floor. In that moment of hesitation, Lyu brings her wooden sword crashing mercilessly into the side of his face.

My own face twitches as I watch his massive body crash against a wall, blood spurting from his nose as his face meets the hard surface.

"Uh…wait! Please wait!"

I'm left alone now, and I cry out as Lyu charges toward me.

I don't want to fight. I want to listen. I want to hear your story in your own words.

Those are the only thoughts on my mind as I stand blocking her way forward.

"You're in my way."

She doesn't seem to have the time for any of that.

She narrows her blue eyes deep within her hood, and the next moment, the delicate foot inside her boot is stomping the ground.

"?!"

She's just leaped over my head.

—She's outwitted me!!

I'm amazed that she was able to take the last of her momentum and use it to clear my head, barely grazing my hair. She doesn't turn around when she lands on the other side—just takes off running like the wind.

"After her, Rabbit Foot!!" Bors yells as he peels his head from the wall.

I hear his angry voice battering my back; I have the highest ability of anyone in the hunting party, and he wants me to pursue her.

Practically before he's finished his sentence, I'm kicking my own feet against the crystal floor to pursue Lyu for my own reasons.

"Yaaa!!"

Already, I can barely make out her long cape. I race after her as she chases the catman. A moment later, she disappears, probably because she's turned a corner in the passageway.

I come to a halt before the multitude of branching passages, unsure where to go. Very quickly, though, I make my choice. The one I choose echoes with the menacing roars and screams of monsters. Following what I assume to be the cries of the beasts that have met with Lyu's sword, I keep running. As if to confirm my guess, I pass the writhing bodies of monsters she has cast aside and piles of ash arranged like footprints.

There's a limit to this method, though, and soon enough I've completely lost track of the incredibly fast elf within the massive Dungeon.

"Where did she go…?"

My sense of urgency increases the panic I feel, and an uncomfortable sweat covers my body.

At that very moment, I hear a song.

"Now, far away—in the infinite heavens—"

I stop in my tracks.

The fragments of song continue to echo from somewhere in the Dungeon, unconcerned with me.

"Come to my foolish self—to the one who has abandoned you—"

Magical power swells.

My adventurer's intuition quivers in fear as the reverberations from some kind of bombardment reach me, even from a distance, like water overflowing from a vessel.

And then, it is clear that the magical power has reached its critical point.

"Pregnant with the light of stardust, defeat your enemy!"

No way!!

My intuition was right.

"Luminous Wind!!"

There's a thundering noise, and the passageway in front of me is blasted apart.

"?!"

A huge ball of light crosses the path before me, bringing with it a storm of wind.

I throw my arms in front of my face as a meteor shower of debris flies from right to left.

Along with the savage roar of magical power, the Dungeon fills with screams.

"…It pierced the Dungeon walls?"

I shake off my surprise at this ridiculous power and walk into the newly formed tunnel. Strangely enough, the track of the explosion leads me to Lyu.

Once I make my way past four crumbled crystal walls, I find myself in an enormous room. There's a lot of dry land, but a number of waterways also flow into the space. Perhaps due to the lingering heat from the huge ball of magical light, steam is rising from the water and forming a light mist.

As I burst through the broken wall into this room, I find the catman at my feet, curled insect-like into a ball.

"You…"

"…R-Rabbit Foot? H-help me! Save me from her!!"

Of course I don't need to ask who he means by *her.*

All of a sudden, the faint shadow of a humanoid form steps out of the mist in the center of the room and comes into focus.

It's an elf, a wooden sword in her hand and a perilous look in her eyes.

"Miss Lyu…!" I cry out, squinting.

"…So you've followed me here, have you, Mr. Cranell?"

Lyu looks at me with her sharp gaze, as if she's just noticed I'm here.

That alone is enough to make me unsure what to say. I almost miss the words she whispers from behind her mask.

"…Why are you always doing this?"

Then, more loudly—

"Move over. You're in the way. I can't get to him with you there."

She looks past me to the catman.

Brandishing her bloodied sword, she slowly approaches us, her long boots scraping the ground loudly.

The catman, still crouched on the ground, groans at the terrifying sight.

"My only mistake was that I didn't put an end to you last time. I was arrogant to assume I'd killed you without properly checking, and I regret that."

Lyu's voice is full of resentment as she curses her own poor work. The whole time she's reciting this monologue, her eyes are piercing the catman.

"…I should have made sure you were dead that time."

As the word *dead* falls from her lips, I almost faint. Like her cold, clouded eyes, her face has changed.

It's not the face of the serious elf who worked at the tavern nor of the gallant adventurer who came to our rescue so many times.

It is the face of an avenger.

Is this really Lyu?

No, this is…

…*Gale Wind?*

When we were on the eighteenth floor together, she told me something about her past. Now the character from that story seems to have appeared before me. A different elf, one I've never met before.

"But we'll clear that debt here and now—your calculations and all," Lyu says resolutely as she pulls the mask from her face.

The catman screams as she walks steadily toward him, as if he can no longer stand his own terror.

"Rabbit Foot! Kill her; I'm begging you! It's awful; my whole body hurts; the blood won't stop…! The arm she cut off…!"

He seems to be in anguish as he hugs his bleeding body with his remaining arm. I shiver as I stare at Lyu's dagger.

"I-is it true? That you cut off this man's arm…?"

"…Yes, I was the one who severed his arm. I sliced off his ear, too. And what of it?!"

Anger and regret are blended inseparably in her voice. She has clearly confessed her deeds. I sink to the floor as my knees collapse beneath me.

"Move aside immediately!"

"M-Miss Ly—"

"I said move!!"

The tip of the wooden sword is pointing at me.

Her rage is enough to make me shrink, Level Four or not. The heartbeat thundering in my ears and the sweat pouring from me are near their peak.

"If you interfere, I'll throw you aside, too…I don't have time for it."

Her words freeze my throat.

"Please, Rabbit Foot...Save meee...!"

The catman's wail drives my anxiety even higher.

In front of me is an ultimatum, behind me a plea.

It's just like a scene in a drama. There's the criminal starving for blood, and here, facing her, is the detective, and there the victim pleading for help.

It's me, in the role of detective, who's been driven relentlessly into a corner. What a poor actor I am. Or to borrow the words of the deities, how wretchedly I have been miscast in this role.

I can hardly bring myself to watch.

"...Please tell me."

Although I feel on the verge of being crushed, I draw up all my emotional strength and speak.

I have to know. I have to understand.

The whole story, and Lyu's true intentions.

If I don't, I'll never be able to arrive at an answer.

So I buck this tremendous pressure and ask her.

"Did you kill the man from Rivira?"

"I don't have time to answer your questions!"

"A body was found outside Rivira! People saw you fleeing the scene!"

"How many times do I have to say it for you to understand?!"

She's full of irritation, determined not to give in.

"Miss Lyu, I'm begging you! Please answer me!!"

I pour all my yearning to hear her side of the story into my next four words.

"Did you kill him?!"

"It wasn't me!!"

We're yelling so loudly it's like we're fighting.

My eyes meet the sky-blue ones that have lost their calm.

Her shout is like that of a frenzied criminal.

The bitter words hurled at me contain no explanation or excuse, only emotion.

But—it's enough.

"...I understand."

At least for me.

"Rabbit Foot, what are you doing? Hurry up and save me! Hurry up and...?"

The catman is screaming at me as I let the tension drain from my body.

My physical body is still standing opposite her, but in my heart, I'm no longer opposing her.

Jura notices the change.

The scene is no longer composed of a criminal, a detective, and a victim.

Instead, there are two detectives and one true criminal.

And Jura knows it.

"Will you show me your wounds?" I ask him calmly.

"Huh? What are you talking about...?"

"Please show me where your arm was cut."

It just so happens that I very, very recently saw a man whose arm had been cut off—the elf Luvis, who had been attacked by the moss huge.

I didn't want to look at it, but the wound where the monster tore his arm off was really awful. The endless blood, the clothes and equipment stained deep red, the overwhelmingly strong smell of fresh blood.

The sight of his severed arm was so awful I felt the blood drain from my head the moment I glimpsed it.

But this guy *doesn't have any of those symptoms.*

Sure, his clothes and equipment are covered in blood, but not so much that it would cause irreversible necrosis of the upper arm. The smell of fresh blood that invades one's nostrils is missing, too.

That's what my memory has been trying to tell me all along. That's the sense of incongruence that was flashing in my mind.

Until a minute ago, I'd been so upset I hadn't realized.

But now I see.

That missing arm—

"That wound…*It's old, isn't it?*"

He glares at me angrily.

Lyu said she herself severed his arm and sliced off his ear. But what if she did it in the past, when she was fully consumed by her desire for revenge—during that regrettable period of time she told me about with such grief on the eighteenth floor?

It makes sense. And it explains a few things.

This catman got upset and refused treatment for his wounds. Could that have been because he was worried about what we would discover if we examined his body? Was he afraid we would notice his wounds were old?

In other words, he *inflicted his fresh wounds himself.*

Lyu hasn't even attacked him yet.

There are some other odd things as well.

Actually, quite a lot about this whole situation strikes me as unnatural.

If Lyu was using magic to cause explosions, then her victims would all have burns on them. But that didn't hold true for one of them: the dwarf I encountered.

He alone was marked with dagger wounds and nothing else.

I'm guessing that dwarf was the only one of Lyu's enemies whose whereabouts she discovered. And she probably took out her weapon because he resisted.

"I've been thinking this for a while now…but your claims don't add up."

"What are you talking about? I explained…!"

"Okay then, why are you *alive* right now?"

"…?!"

"If your arm was cut off, your ear was cut off, and you were the victim of magic…why are you not dead?"

His opponent is Gale Wind.

She destroyed a massive faction single-handedly. She is a legendary Level Four warrior with a bounty on her head.

It doesn't make sense that she would capture him but let him escape in the end.

"At first I thought maybe she was deranged...because there's no way Lyu would leave that place where Bors and the other adventurers had gathered after she had attacked you."

That is, if they were indeed attacked, as this man claimed.

Why would Lyu create an explosion but then purposely not put an end to things?

—Because she hadn't been attacking anyone in the first place.

Why hadn't we found any signs of magical power or heard any spells, like I did this time?

—Because she hadn't been blowing up the floor.

So what's the big picture?

Even this miscast detective can figure that out.

The answer is simple.

Everything is a performance created and acted out by these people.

"I found this in the other passageway."

I flip the scarlet fragment toward him. It's still giving off heat, and I've seen that before.

"It's an Inferno Stone, isn't it?" I say.

I think back to something that happened four months ago, right after I met Welf. He'd brought me to see his workshop, and he showed me a device made for use in the furnace. In order to forge minerals from the Dungeon, he had to use a powerful explosive that enhanced the heat of the flames.

The catman's face twitches.

"Miss Lyu said she didn't kill anyone...and I believe her."

The only thing I still don't understand is the murder on the eighteenth floor.

If her rage truly drove her to kill that man...

I need to know the answer to this last question.

If she has once again reverted to a blood-soaked avenger, then all my reasoning will crumble under the force of her overwhelming desire to kill.

—It wasn't even justice.

Lyu once said those words to me, her voice filled with regret.

"Mr. Cranell…"

But Lyu said she didn't do it.

She told me that with unclouded eyes—eyes filled with an elf's fierce pride, hatred of lies, and strong sense of duty. With the sky-blue eyes I know so well.

That was enough. More than enough.

With my back to the catman, I turn my face toward him and stare intently.

"If Lyu isn't the one who caused the explosions…then it could only have been you and your gang."

All the explosions so far have been their destructive work.

I still don't know why they're blowing up this floor. But finally, all the different strands have come together in a single rope.

"Please show me the wound on your arm."

If he shows me that, I'll feel sure.

Show me the wound she gave you as proof of her guilt.

I'm aware that my own eyes are cold, red, and glittering.

I scowl at him, speaking in a tone that leaves no room for argument.

Lyu is staring at me, the one person who believes her.

The catman gulps.

Then, unmistakably, he clicks his tongue.

As he glares at me, the drained face of a severely wounded victim transforms into that of a brutal villain.

The next instant, the hand that had been stretched out by his side flashes forward.

"So I've been discovered!"

"Ah!"

I fly back to avoid the stroke of red that suddenly cuts through the air.

He is gripping a scarlet whip in his left hand.

"You and those idiots from Rivira are worthless! Even if you didn't kill Leon, I thought you'd at least slow her down!"

"Jura…!"

Lyu and I are standing side by side facing our opponent. He rests the whip on his shoulder, then draws an elixir from his pouch, deftly removes the lid with his single hand, and pours it over his head. The top-grade item heals his bloody self-inflicted wounds and sends smoke rising from the scars.

"Turk did well, but he slipped up at the end. He got nervous about you, Leon, and let off the explosion too soon."

Like a magician giving away his secrets, he throws the Inferno Stones he'd been hiding onto the ground around us.

There must be at least twenty of them. He definitely could have caused that much damage to the Dungeon with this many stones.

"I'm sorry, Miss Lyu, for doubting you even a little…!"

"…No, I got hotheaded and wasn't discreet enough. I was trying to avoid you for your own sake…but I was wrong."

We're talking side by side, without looking at each other. Lyu mutters softly to me, her eyes glued to the man in front of us.

"Thank you, Mr. Cranell, for believing in a fool like me. I am deeply grateful."

I'm not sure if it's joy or happiness, but warmth floods my chest.

"I want to stop this villain…Please, help me."

"Of course!"

I nod, a smile spreading over my face as I continue to look forward. Keeping my gaze carefully fixed on our enemy, I draw the Divine Knife.

"Jura, accept your fate. You very nearly incited the people of Rivira to kill me, but your plans have crumbled. You have no one left."

Taming her rage with reason, Lyu speaks to Jura as if she is delivering a final decree. Her eyes drilling into him, she slowly closes the gap between him and us.

In response, he smiles.

Then, brandishing his scarlet whip, he laughs at us.

"Ha-ha-ha-ha, heh-heh-heh...! Don't make me laugh!"

"..."

"Have you forgotten, Leeeon?"

Lyu's rival—her sworn enemy—lets out another loud laugh.

An instant later, the whip lashes against the ground, gleaming with a scarlet light.

"I am a tamer!"

A second later, a massive shadow breaks through the ceiling and falls to the ground.

"Huh?!"

Both Lyu and I kick off the ground. She leaps to the left and I to the right; the enormous form crashes right between us. As the whole room shakes, I throw my arms in front of my face to block the flying fragments of crystal.

"Meet my pet."

Astonished, I look up at an enormous writhing body.

Its gaping maw is searching for anything whatsoever to gulp down.

The long, swollen form has no arms or legs. Where the face should be, there are three pairs of eyes.

It's a gigantic multi-eyed serpent.

"What the hell are you doing?" Aisha asked, her fearless smile belying her words. She glared at Turk and his companions as they *drew their swords while lunging at her.*

"So it wasn't just one of them..." Welf said.

"Yeah, seems all of them were on the dark side," Ouka answered. As their four opponents drew their weapons and exchanged murderous glances, the two young men pulled out their own weapons.

The enemy party was comprised of two humans and two animal people. All but Turk were wearing large packs. All four had finally shown their true colors.

"Since we're pressed for time and you won't leave us alone...we'll kill you here! For the sake of Jura's plan, of course!"

The next instant, Turk pulled out a scarlet whip and summoned a monster.

"?!"

Aisha and the rest of the party leaped back as its long body burst through a wall. Lilly gripped Daphne and Haruhime gripped Mikoto, and the four fled the crumbling passage.

Strangely enough, at the very same moment that Bell and Lyu were facing the huge serpent, another of the same monster was appearing before the rest of his party.

"What the...?!"

"A lambton...!"

The long, massive serpent is an extreme large-category monster, definitely imposing enough to be a floor boss. It measures around five meders high and at least ten long.

For a second, my mind goes blank before the overwhelming presence of the beast.

Despite its awesome appearance, I can't recall anything about the monster before my eyes. Even when Lyu shouts what must be its name, I can't remember anything. What happened to all that information Eina drilled into me before I left on our expedition for the lower levels?

"—Oh yeah."

Finally, from the depths of my memory, I manage to extract some information. The instant I do, my breath stops.

"No way...!"

"Ouranos."

The black-clad figure gripping a crystal ball spoke into the surface of the magic item.

"As you expected, I have discovered a storeroom full of monsters."

"Are any Xenos imprisoned there?"

"No, none. Just ordinary monsters."

The figure talking with Ouranos was his closest assistant, the eight-hundred-year-old fallen sage, Fels. The mage had used special powers to invade Knossos on a top secret mission and was now reporting back via an oculus.

"It seems they were transporting other types of monsters captured in the Dungeon as well, not just Xenos."

"How many?"

"Let's just say there are too many for me to count."

The cold stone room was filled with black cages of varying sizes containing different kinds of monsters. There was a plant-type monster with yellow-green skin, a group of large-category monsters captured as a herd, and a dragon with drool dripping from its razor-toothed maw. They seemed to have been suppressed with some kind of tranquilizer, perhaps a magic item, so that even when Fels drew close, they reacted only dully.

The mage held a magic-stone lamp up to the cages one by one. Even without human flesh, the wise skeleton felt a vague chill.

"Are Lido and the others with you?" Ouranos asked.

"No, we split up. Some of the Xenos were imprisoned like this in the past. Even if they're not of the same species, I decided it wouldn't be a pleasant experience for them to witness this…Also, the enemy's attacks are quite brutal."

"Can you dispose of them?"

Glancing over a hastily drawn-up list of the monsters, Fels answered Ouranos in a straightforward manner.

"To be honest, it would be difficult. Their numbers aside, quite a few of them are hard-to-handle specimens."

Most of the middle- and lower-level monsters generally considered formidable were represented in the group. The documents Fels had discovered suggested that *Ikelos Familia* and other Evils' Remnants had been conducting some sort of experiment on them.

Fels stopped in front of several large cages at the back of the hall.

"All the same, this is hard to believe…"

The voice that came from the depths of the black hood was part moan, part whisper.

"I didn't expect them to have brought up *monsters from the deep levels…*"

There were two enormous cages. The bars of both had been bent out of shape from the inside.

CHAPTER 4 COUNTDOWN

"Ha-ha-ha-ha-ha-ha-ha-ha-ha-ha!!"

The catman's laughter echoes through the room.

As Lyu and I stand side by side watching, a large drop of sticky liquid falls from the serpent monster's pointed fang.

It's a lambton.

A rare monster from the *deep levels.* Its head narrows toward the tip, and its jaws—which open vertically—look wide enough to swallow an orc whole. On either side of its mouth are nine holes comprising an organ not seen on other monsters.

But the first thing I notice is the man-made collar attached below its head. It sparkles with a red jewel that seems to mark it as the tamer's "pet."

Its skin is deep blue, and its amber eyes roll restlessly in its head as it glares at Lyu and me.

"How did a monster from the deep levels get all the way up here...?!"

For a monster from so far down in the depths of the Dungeon to appear here in the Water Capital is a very unusual irregularity indeed. As I gape in shock at the unbelievable phenomenon, the catman smiles jeeringly at us.

"I brought it from Knossos. It's one of the monsters the crew over there captured. You probably know what I'm talking about, since you were mixed up with those creepy talking monsters and *Ikelos Familia.*"

"...!"

He sounds like he knows all about my connections with the Xenos and *Ikelos Familia.* And if that man-made dungeon has something to do with this, then everything is starting to make sense. Still, a monster this huge would surely catch the attention of other adventurers. But there haven't been any rumors about this, let alone a single report of a sighting. Strange!

My thoughts must be showing on my face, because the catman continues talking, his expression still as relaxed as ever.

"You haven't heard about it, Rabbit Foot? The special ability of the wormwells?"

"...!"

"'Lambton' is just a nickname, like the ones we adventurers have."

Now I remember.

I mentally run through the information about deep-level monsters that I reviewed in one of the illustrated books I studied with Eina before the expedition, just in case.

"Lambton" is the nickname adventurers have given the species. Its proper name is wormwell, the first part meaning "serpent" and the second referring to a "water well." As I recall with a jolt of surprise why this is its name, Lyu draws her brows together and says what I'm thinking.

"Lambtons are able to *move between floors* by boring through the earth...!"

"A monster that moves between floors?!" Welf shouted in response to Aisha's explanation, completely forgetting his surroundings.

"Yeah, that's why it has that over-the-top nickname, 'lambton.' The written characters for it mean 'evil omen.'"

They were in a passageway on the twenty-fifth floor. As the party faced the same type of monster Bell was encountering two floors down, Aisha smiled nervously.

Normally, the wormwell—or lambton—lived on the thirty-seventh floor. But just as its name suggested, it had the ability to bore vertically upward through the floors, as if it were digging a well in reverse, *and appear on the higher floors*. That's what made it so terrifying to adventurers.

"You mean a monster from the lower floors can invade the higher ones...?!"

For wormwells, that wasn't an irregular characteristic; it was simply their nature. They paid no attention to the principle of levels and instead moved freely between floors. Mikoto and Chigusa, who understood exactly how terrifying this was, turned pale.

"So just how strong is it...?" Lilly squeaked, stunned by this encounter with a totally unexpected monster.

According to the Guild, it had a potential of Level Four.

It only rarely appeared in the lower levels, but when it did, it was as good as a death knell announcing total destruction to adventurers.

"You must be kidding!!" Welf barked, holding his greatsword at the ready.

Under the control of Turk and his scarlet whip, the growling wormwell slowly twisted its body into an attack position.

As nervous tension rippled through the party, Aisha shouted out a warning.

"Whatever you do, don't cling onto that monster! If you do, it will carry you to another floor!"

What she didn't say was that most likely, before the unfortunate adventurer got there, they would be ground to mincemeat between the monster's massive body and the rocky walls of the Dungeon tunnel it crawled through.

In either case, the moment the monster captured you, you were done for.

"Get 'em, lambton!"

The werewolf Turk beat his whip against the ground. In response, the giant serpent growled loudly, then lunged toward the party.

"Aaaaaaaaaaaaaaaaaaaaaaaaaaaaaaaaaaaaaaaaaaaaa!!"

"Aaah!"

I leap to avoid the wormwell's darting head.

With a shiver, I realize it can easily reach every corner of this huge room, which measures around twenty meders high and fifty across. The serpent's slithering body shaves off crystals and clusters from the floor and sends them flying. Meanwhile, a wave from the turbulent waterway splashes over me.

But even as I'm drenched from head to toe, I never take my eyes off the writhing monster on the far side of the room.

"It's way stronger than anything on the twenty-seventh floor…!"

The wormwell seems to mysteriously appear from its habitat on the thirty-seventh floor, and then disappear again without a trace. It never burrows down below the thirty-seventh floor, though. That's because it would be suicide to go even one level down in the Dungeon, where monsters grow stronger the deeper one descends.

I've heard that many a party of adventurers has been wiped out when this monster with its disproportionate potential appeared on a higher floor. I even seem to recall hearing that the wormwell is the most feared of all creatures among adventurers who explore the lower levels.

The distinct sound it makes as it burrows through the ground foretells disaster. It is indeed an evil omen.

All the same, it's unprecedented for a wormwell to appear in the Water Capital!!

The highest floor it's ever been sighted on is the twenty-ninth. Eina told me that it would be impossible for a lambton to burrow through ten floors' worth of solid rock.

But things are falling into place now.

That huge hole I discovered with Bors's party was made by this monster. It was the track the thing made *as it moved between floors*!

"Sic 'em, lambton!"

The catman tamer lashes his whip against the ground. As soon as he does, the lambton roars and hurls its body into the air.

"Wha—?"

Its head draws a ten-meder-high arc through space. Its long body follows, swimming through the air with flashes of deep blue. I'm captivated for a moment by the fantastic sight, monster or not. Time seems to slow down. Even as it does, though, my instincts are screaming out a warning.

The body twists, and slowly the menacing form is drawn downward by gravity. A black shadow blocks out the white crystal lights on the ceiling, darkening the spot where I stand.

I look up in shock as the serpent's huge body spins downward toward me.

"Run, Mr. Cranell!"

Lyu's voice pushes me into motion, and I rush away from the falling form with all my strength.

"————————————!!"

The room—no, more likely the entire Dungeon—shakes with a thundering crash as the lambton smashes onto the floor where I was standing a second before.

I'm thrown into the air by the shock waves, and my vision blurs.

The serpent is twisting and burrowing its way into the rock floor. Even as my body flies over the crystals, the long form is swallowed completely by the ground.

Using the momentum from my rolling landing, I quickly stand up and manage to recover a fighting stance. My blood runs cold as I look around the room now disfigured by a gigantic hole.

"...?!"

"...!"

Lyu and I both aim our weapons at the ground.

The vibrations emanating upward are ceaseless. The serpent is digging through the ground with the intention of swallowing its prey—us—whole.

Where will it reappear?

From land or from water?

"Wrong!" The catman jeers as we stare warily at the ground.

The next instant, the huge form emerges with a crushing noise off to *one side*. Crystal fragments fly from a wall near Lyu on the west side of the room, and the lambton lunges forward with its jaws open wide.

"Miss Lyu!!"

"Yaaa!"

Lyu seems to be on fire as the serpent bears down on her. To make up for lost time, she kicks the ground and, with a swish of her long cape, flies upward. She's deftly taken refuge in the air as the long body races past below.

She lands next to me and takes in the monster that is now charging across the center of the room.

"Are lambtons always this insane?" I ask, panting.

"Well, since they're a rare monster, I've only encountered the species one other time. I can't really answer your question…" she replies vaguely, readying her wooden sword.

The only time I've ever confronted a monster this huge was when I fought the Goliath. But this thing…Both its attack methods and its scale are crazy. I guess that's what deep-level monsters are like!

"So the end has come, eh, Leon? You and Rabbit Foot can get real close inside this guy's stomach!"

The catman laughs loudly.

"We don't need to take part in our enemy's circus performance," Lyu whispers into my shoulder.

I'm surprised, but I nod quickly. After exchanging these brief words, we start running forward in parallel.

I extend my right hand toward the roaring lambton.

"Firebolt!"

The electrifying flames that burst from my fist reach the monster's face and land on one of the nine holes next to its mouth. Of course, this magic attack doesn't inflict much damage on my extreme large-category opponent.

Still, the three pairs of bloodshot eyes focus in on me.

Gotcha!

The monster's angry shriek makes me sweat, but nevertheless, I form my hand into a fist.

This is my first fight with a tamer, but even I can figure out that it makes more sense to aim for the tamer himself than for the monster he's controlling. Given that they have to learn tamer skills, my guess is they're often weaker than other adventurers.

So you separate them from their monster and attack them in their "naked" state.

In this case, I'll serve as the bait to draw away the monster while Lyu acts as the spear that pierces the tamer.

As the lambton momentarily focuses its attention on me, Lyu speeds up.

Like a falcon gliding across the open sky, she races forward, body tilted toward the ground. She slips through the narrow gap between the monster's body and the ground and arrives next to the tamer, who had been obstructed by the serpent.

"Jura!"

"Eh?!"

His voice in response to her call is pitiful. Nevertheless, he twists his face into a smile and brings the whip in his single hand down onto the ground.

"!!"

"Huh?!"

To my surprise, the lambton—which I thought was focused on me—whips its head around toward the catman. Having reversed direction, it aims straight for Lyu's back.

"Miss Lyu!"

"?!"

Just before her wooden sword makes contact with the tamer, Lyu is forced to leap back to avoid the lunging monster.

Jura leers at her as she just barely dodges the serpent's fangs. The lambton does not harm its tamer but instead coils around him exactly like it's protecting him.

"Ha-ha-ha…! So you thought you could aim for me, eh? You thought I wasn't ready for that?"

"…!"

"I've imprinted this behavior on my pet quite well!" he brags, still smiling, as Lyu bites her lip.

Meanwhile, I'm blatantly showing my astonishment.

I'm not that familiar with tamers or their profession. I haven't even seen *Ganesha Familia*'s Monsterphilia, so I have no idea how versatile they might be.

Still…this monster seems incredibly well trained!

All I know is what Eina taught me, but my understanding is that essentially, taming monsters doesn't so much involve getting them to do what you want as preventing them from rebelling. It's about making them realize and submit to the superior strength of the tamer—in other words, taming is a skill of submission.

Evidence of that can be found in the fact that tamed monsters will still attack people other than their tamer. I've also heard it's extremely difficult to teach them multiple commands.

But this catman is controlling the monster like it's an extension of his own hands and feet.

"Miss Lyu…Is this guy really such an amazing tamer?"

"No…I mean, he's one of the better ones, but I think he's below *Ganesha Familia* tamers. That is, the Jura Harma I knew five years ago was."

I can't hide my surprise at the fact that Lyu—who is both connected to his faction and is an old rival of this man—also expected his skills to be lower.

The tamer strokes the serpent's slippery body tenderly.

"Ah, shit…It's useless…I'm still afraid! Leon, disgusting Gale Wind!" he shouts, unable to conceal the shaking in his voice.

"Look at this trembling hand! It's like a leaf in the wind! You almost killed me once—of course I'm scared of you!"

That's when I realize.

His smile of a moment before was fake and forced.

"I remember, Leon! I can't forget. There's no way I'd forget!"

"…"

"When I close my eyes, I still see you there, thrashing around in a sea of blood the day you attacked my home! I dream about it every day. I haven't had a good night's sleep since that day! Can you believe it? Not for five years!"

"…?!"

"That day, I hid among the bodies of my slaughtered companions, delirious! I lay there holding my breath and listening to you roar like a monster until you blew our whole home away with your magic! It's strange I even survived."

Lyu stands silent as he lays his feelings out in the open. I'm in a confused panic. I can glimpse his sick emotions now and then in the pair of sunken, wide-open eyes. Not only his severed right arm but even his left arm twitches in reaction to Gale Wind's slightest movement.

I finally get it.

This man's display of fear throughout the performances and destructive schemes he used to fool Bors and the rest of us wasn't an act. The reason I didn't initially question his terror was because it was real.

For him, Lyu is a symbol of trauma.

Gale Wind—the elf who severed his arm, sliced off his ear, and brought him to the brink of death—is more frightening than anyone or anything else.

"If I had to face you alone, I'd piss my pants. That's why I got the monster to fight in my place! It's stronger than I am, this cute little pet of mine!"

Still shaking from uncontrollable fear, the tamer cracks his whip. The lambton lunges at us again, baring its fangs.

The catman laughs as we scramble to defend ourselves from the monster under his command. Meanwhile, the monster moves with great precision and swiftness according to his tamer's will, both attacking and defending.

But I doubt the catman's skills are solely responsible for all this.

No—it has something to do with the circlet around its neck and the scarlet whip. They're magic items.

"Get 'em, lambton!"

At the sound of the werewolf Turk's voice and the crack of his whip, the wormwell charged forward.

In the face of its unstoppable advance, Aisha chose to retreat.

"Get into that side passage!"

Lilly and the others dove in just in time to avoid the wriggling mass heading for them, crushing the narrow passage as it went.

A loud scraping noise filled the corridor they had just left as the bluish-white body slithered across the floor. The screams of monsters crushed beneath its belly echoed down the passage.

Haruhime went pale, overtaken by visceral disgust.

"All this thing has to do is rush us…" Welf screamed.

"…and we're done for!" Ouka yelled back, finishing his thought. Both were staring at the fissures spreading through the entrance to the passage as the enemy charged forward.

It had quickly turned back and was now heading for the panicked party.

"We can't fight it here! Retreat!"

They would be at an enormous disadvantage fighting an extreme large-category monster in their current location. Aisha—who had frequently fought in the deep levels where *Ishtar Familia* headed on its expeditions—quickly gave up on an immediate battle and instead put all her energy into escape.

"Hey, shrimp, find us a field!" she shouted.

"A field?! What do you mean?!" Lilly shouted back, changing color.

"A dead-end room on the twenty-fifth floor! As long as there's not a waterway in it, it will have a field! Take us there!"

In other words, Lilly needed to look at the map.

The party retreated as fast as it could, managing to dull the lambton's movements through repeated shots from Mikoto's and Chigusa's arrows and Daphne's magic dagger.

"Hey, it's not following us. It disappeared!!" Welf shouted, glancing back over his shoulder.

"No, Sir Welf…It's still here!" Mikoto answered, using her Yatano Black Crow skill.

"It burrowed underground! It's coming up from under—No, from the side!! Shoot it!" Aisha screamed at the top of her lungs, sensing the vibrations.

A second later, the lambton burst through the wall next to them and lunged forward.

"Ooooooooooooooooooooooooooooooooooooooo!!"

"Aaaaaaaaaaaaaaaaaaaaaaaaaaaaaaaaaaaaaaaah?!"

"This thing is crazy!"

"Are the deep levels full of this kind of monster?!"

Haruhime's scream, Daphne's desperate shout, and Ouka's horrified question filled the passageway as they just barely evaded the serpent. By this point Haruhime was no more than baggage slowing down the group, so Aisha told her to drop her backpack and slung her over her right shoulder. She clicked her tongue as she glanced back at the approaching monster.

We've been totally prevented from following those adventurers. Bell Cranell asked us to keep an eye on them, but we're really in a tight corner now!

Cursing herself internally, the group's only second-tier adventurer searched for some way out.

Meanwhile, back in the passageway that Aisha and the others had fled, Turk and his three companions were celebrating.

"Ha-ha-ha...! This magic item is amazing! I can't believe I can make even deep-level monsters obey me...Thank you, Evils!"

Turk looked down at the scarlet whip with the jewel fixed to the end, drunk on a false sense of omnipotence. The magic item had been created by the Evils' Remnants hiding out in Knossos. The mysterious crystal—or more accurately, the cursed lump—had been conceived as a way to convince buyers of Xenos and other monsters smuggled for profit by *Ikelos Familia* hunters that the "product" they were buying was safe.

By attaching matching collars to the monsters, the forbidden magic items allowed less-powerful tamers, or even those with no ability at all, to subordinate the creatures. Jura had taken advantage of the recent events in Knossos to smuggle out all these valuable items, which were extremely effective but could not be mass-produced.

"When I heard Jura's plan, I thought he was crazy...But it can fly. If they work this well, it can fly!"

The young werewolf—who had originally belonged to a band of small-time criminals who had nothing to do with the Evils—had sniffed out something lucrative in the last remaining member of *Rudra Familia*, Jura. Now that he saw the effects of the magic item with his own eyes, he was ready to swear his allegiance.

He was determined not only to frame Jura's old enemy, Gale Wind, but also to make sure the catman's whole plan came to fruition.

"Now's our chance to act! Do what Jura commanded!"

The three adventurers wearing backpacks nodded.

Leaving behind the lambton as their parting gift, the party left the scene.

"Haruhime, we need Level Boosts! Start chanting!" Aisha ordered.

"Do you mean Kokonoe? For Lady Mikoto and everyone?"

"Two is enough! If you exhaust yourself now, we'll be in trouble later. For now, just boost Ignis and Masuratakeo on the front line!"

The party had arrived in a dead-end room thanks to Lilly's directions. As soon as they got there, Aisha had started spitting out orders, including one to boost the levels of Welf and Ouka. She was the only one among them with experience exploring the deep levels, and she hadn't allowed Lilly or Daphne to take command. Their situation was too critical—as was clear from Aisha's harsh tone. Plus, she had a detailed understanding of the party's internal balance, gained from her usual non-commander position.

"First that enhanced species, now this…I sure don't get bored when I'm with you guys!" she joked, shaping her mouth into a smile as she brandished her great *podao*.

"I never dreamed the Amazonian Berbera would be saying those words!"

"Yeah, it sure is unexpected…An honor, should we say?"

Ouka and Welf bantered with her as the particles of light from Haruhime's Level Boost encircled them. They stood on either side of Aisha, holding their greatsword, ax, and shields at the ready.

With their strongest forces at the forefront, the group was prepared to fight the deep-level monster.

"…Is this the calamity?"

"Cassandra, snap out of it!"

As the prophetess of tragedy stood in a daze, the curtain lifted on the battle.

"—!!"

As if resonating with the serpent's roar, the collar around its neck pulsated with light, and the beast trembled.

"It was a real pain to get this thing onto this floor."

Lyu and I frantically dodge as the lambton twists its long body and attacks viciously, responding to the crack of the whip on the ground.

"Granted, it was able to dig its way here itself, but the problem was that body. It's just so easy to spot. I had to make it swallow any adventurers who saw it."

"...!"

"The hardest part was getting it out of Knossos."

The catman glances at me as I tighten my fists in response to his casual confession to murder.

"Rabbit Foot, after you tangled with *Ikelos Familia*, I decided I'd better get out of Knossos. Thanks to you—no, it started when Dix messed up—I figured the Guild would eventually reach my hideout. And they did!" Jura shouted. "Once the place we'd been quietly hiding in was gone, there was no guarantee we'd be safe...That's when I started moving forward with my plan."

A shock wave from the serpent's movements sends me flying. As I land, I look over my shoulder and ask him a question.

"From then?!"

"Yeah. You didn't think we'd managed to move the monsters down here since yesterday, all with Leon chasing us, did you? We started by hiding two lambtons on this floor."

"Wha...?"

"See, as long as we kept them quiet under the water, none of the other adventurers would find them. Oh, and who knows? Turk and his guys might be attacking the adventurers right now. 'Cause I gave them one of these here whips."

"...!"

As I absorb these shocking words, the catman continues.

"Then two days ago, when the forces finally swarmed into Knossos, we were about to push our plans forward and hightail it out of Knossos... But Leon happened to be in the group, and she spotted me."

His eyes are filled with a deep hatred as he glares at Lyu.

"She kept chasing me, so I used Jan and Turk to do something about her. I knew she'd follow us onto this floor, so I lit a fire under the people in Rivira in order to stop her."

I'm guessing that when he temporarily evaded Lyu and escaped from Knossos to the eighteenth floor, his first step was to send his two underlings to Rivira. But one of them was captured and questioned by Lyu, leading her to head as quickly as possible to the twenty-seventh floor.

And then Turk, who had escaped her notice...must have decided to make use of his friend. He killed the injured Jan, making it look like Gale Wind was the murderer, and ran to tell Bors and me in Rivira. After that, he spearheaded the formation of a hunting party to pursue Gale Wind, just as the catman had ordered him to.

All of this is mere speculation on my part, but it nevertheless makes me sick to my stomach. And I'm fairly sure I must be right.

"I figured I'd use the guys who came with me down to the twenty-seventh floor as decoys to keep you and Leon away from me! But then when the Rivira crew finally got down here, I just blew them all up at once with the explosions!"

"...!"

In other words, he sacrificed his companions in order to keep the residents from Rivira on his side and make them afraid of Gale Wind.

Anger spreads over Lyu's face as she listens to our opponent's clear explanation.

I, too, feel both fear and disgust toward this man who was willing to use any means whatsoever to achieve his ends.

But...why is he telling us all this now? To demonstrate his own calmness? To upset us? Or...to buy time?

As I stand here bewildered, a tail drops down from above my head and crashes into the ground with an even stronger impact than the others so far.

"Argh!"

I jump as far away as I can. As I catch my breath, Lyu lands beside me.

"As I suspected, Jura's been feeding this monster magic stones to enhance it…"

"…!"

Her words make me realize we have a long fight ahead of us. It will be nearly impossible to reach the magic stones inside a body this big. Risking an attempt at a single deadly blow won't work. It probably makes more sense to try to tip the balance with magic, even at the expense of huge mental strain.

Acting as a wall won't work in the face of our opponent's all-out attacks…But what if Lyu and I use Concurrent Casting and Concurrent Charging to turn ourselves into a living fortress? Would the tamer let us get away with pulling off such an obvious strategy…?

I'm drawing on all my past experience to try to come up with the best possible strategy. The next thing Lyu says catches me totally off guard, though.

"…But I've *already figured out* the connection between Jura's commands and the monster's movements."

I can't believe Lyu already understands the behavioral patterns the tamer has imprinted onto his monster—in other words, the relationship between the motions of the whip and the lambton's actions.

How did she figure it out in such a short time?

"One option is to destroy the magic item, but once the monster is freed from its control, it will go wild and that will be a hassle to deal with. I'm going to immobilize it by force."

"Uh, okay, got it! B-b-but how…?!"

"Jura is wary of my magic, so I'll kill it with my weapon."

Ignoring my confusion, Lyu runs her finger down her wooden sword.

"Mr. Cranell, you feint while I kill it."

"O-okay, got it!"

"Its only really troublesome behavior is its ability to burrow underground. If you see it trying to do that, use your Swift-Strike Magic to block it. I believe in you."

The battle-hardened upper-class adventurer speaks unwaveringly even in the face of this overwhelming monster.

"I've fought a lambton before. There's no reason to think it can beat us."

The record that Lyu—or rather *Astrea Familia*—has registered with the Guild is the forty-first floor. She is a truly incredible warrior experienced in fighting in the deep levels. I'm struck by her powers of observation and insight, her intelligence in developing and proposing a strategy without hesitation, and more than anything the determination that underlies her decisions and actions.

I have a long way to go before my ability as an adventurer reaches hers.

"Let's take care of this thing quickly so we can capture Jura."

The flames of rage still burning high in her breast, the elf transforms herself into an arrow of the gale wind.

"!!"

At the same time, I start running in the opposite direction.

The monster's multiple eyes roll around in its head, following both of us as we split off to the left and right.

In order to draw more of its attention toward me, I increase my attacks, using my agility and speed to confuse it.

"Yaaah!"

"Ergh?"

In that window of distraction, Lyu bravely flies toward the enemy's chest.

Anticipating the monster's every move, she dodges each of its defensive strikes within a hairbreadth, channeling the force of her charges into her wooden sword. Scales fly every which way, and the beast's skin grows ragged. The ground vibrates as if she's pounding it with a massive iron hammer, producing a cracking sound that slides past my eardrums.

Meanwhile, I slip Hakugen from my left hand back into its sheath and extend my now-empty hand toward my left leg. Very quietly, I extract several items from my reinforced leg holster and inspect them.

There's a high potion, a magic potion, an antidote, and two vials of Tiger Cub Elixir High Dual Potion.

I don't skimp on the amount I use.

Then I harden my resolve and begin sounding the chime.

Argonaut.

Pure-white particles of light gather around my left hand as I begin the Concurrent Charge.

It would take at least two minutes of charging to take down a large-category monster this big. But my job right now is not to annihilate it. It's to support Lyu!

"Shit! Burrow, lambton!"

The catman, seeing that the monster is suffering under Lyu's attacks, cracks his whip.

It's the command I was expecting.

I instantly thrust out my left hand. I've been charging for twenty seconds.

Aiming for the enemy's head, which is attempting to burrow into the ground as fast as it can, I let out a shout.

"Firebolt!"

A huge bolt of electrical fire surrounded by white particles of light splits the ground between the crystal floor and the lambton.

"OOOOOOOOOOOOOOOOOOOOOOOOO?!"

Thrown backward by the explosion, the serpent writhes on the ground.

Taking advantage of the moment when the beast—having failed in its attempt to burrow—is twisting in agony, Lyu ups the speed of her attacks.

"Whoa?!"

Front, left diagonal, side, diagonal again.

Both the catman and I are gaping at Lyu as she lunges and swerves, unleashing a rapid-fire series of attacks. Her speed increases with each thrust, and now she's moving so fast she practically leaves an afterimage.

If I could see her from above, I'm sure her lunges and retreats would form a five-pointed star enclosing the monster at its center.

The unbroken string of fierce blows from her wooden sword lift our opponent's enormous body off the ground.

There's no mistaking it—as the speed of her attacks increases, so does their ferocity.

"*Yaaaaaaaaaaaaaaaaaaaaaaaaaaaaaaaaaaaaaaaaaaaaaaa!!*"

Her sword glows with the blue-green light of her skill.

Finally, she lands a decisive blow slantwise across its breast, throwing its giant form against the wall.

"————?!"

My eyes are popping out of my head, and the catman's are filled with horror, as if he's watching the return of his worst nightmare.

Did she really just blow away the body of an ultra-high-class monster?

The revolting head and neck, which had been shrieking in agony and convulsing, fall to the ground. Crumbling crystals bury the massive body.

Whether it's dead or just unconscious, I'm too dumbfounded even to cheer Gale Wind's incredible show of skill in knocking out an extreme large-category monster with just her weapon.

I'm guessing the catman—who's rooted to the ground—must be feeling the same way.

"Jura, you're all that's left…It's over."

Lyu brandishes her sword, crosses the now-still room, and walks up to the catman. Coming to my senses, I follow. Quickly refueling with High Dual Potion, I stand by her side facing Jura.

His companions are gone now, and so is the monster he tamed.

He's too traumatized to raise a sword against Lyu.

As she said, this is the end.

His one remaining hand shaking, he drops his eyes before Lyu's piercing gaze.

And then, his hair hiding his eyes—he slowly smiles.

"Frontline forces, stand firm! Just one more!"

Aisha's voice rang through the room.

Welf and Ouka clenched their teeth, held their shields at a slant, and managed to throw the monster off its line of attack. Their whole bodies were strained and blood spurted from their wounds, but their arms and legs, swathed in the light of the Level Boost, showed no sign of giving out. The shields made of hard white valmars, too, stood up to the task. Right away, Cassandra showered them with restorative magic.

The lambton roared in confusion in the face of this defensive wall, which managed to hold the line through raw courage and simple, precise skill no matter how desperately the beast threw itself against them.

Arrows and other sharp weapons pierced the gaping maw even as it howled.

On the top of the mouth were eighteen holes, nine on the left and nine on the right. By now, they were marked with wounds from arrowheads, throwing knives, and Aisha's great *podao*.

These pits gave wormwells an extraordinary ability to sense heat. It was these pits, in fact, that enabled the monsters to accurately locate adventurers even when underground. Because these organs also allowed them to distinguish between humans and monsters by reacting to magic stones and to detect with great sensitivity the use of magic and magic blades, they were able to escape underground as necessary, thus making them extremely hard to combat. Even now, the wormwell was repeatedly burrowing underground, foiling the attempts by Lilly and the others to use their magic blades. Unless Swift-Strike Magic was used, it would likely be difficult to land a blow on the beast.

For all those reasons, Aisha aimed first for the pits on its head.

While Welf and Ouka were literally laying their lives on the line to hold back the enemy's attacks and distract it, Aisha worked with Mikoto and the others in the center guard to destroy the pits.

The dead-end room Lilly had led them to was indeed a field of crystals, with crystal columns sprouting throughout it like groves of trees. There was no such thing as an obstacle for the lambton, which could burrow through Dungeon floors and walls, but the large crystal formations certainly slowed its movements. Mikoto, Chigusa, Lilly, and Daphne rained down their blows onto the impaired monster.

Again and again it fled underground, slowly turning much of the room into a flat plain. Just one pit remained intact on top of its head.

"Eeyaaaaaaaaaaa!!"

"Now, Lady Chigusa!" Mikoto—her quiver already empty—shouted as Ouka and Welf pushed the monster off course.

Chigusa, who was hiding in one of the remaining groves of crystal columns, aimed her taut bow and arrow at the serpent. Only her left eye peeped out from behind her bangs.

Like Mikoto, Chigusa had trained with Takemikazuchi and was an all-around fighter. She was timid and perhaps not well suited to the role of adventurer, but there was one skill in which she surpassed Mikoto: archery.

"Dead-on and deadly—"

Whispering the war god's charm, Chigusa released her bowstring and her concentration simultaneously.

Kokutoba, the arrow Welf had forged for her with his top-class smith's skills, whined through the air and landed square on the lambton's last intact pit.

"?!"

"Yesss!" Aisha cheered, pivoting from defense to offense.

For a lambton, losing the pits on its head was equivalent to being blinded. This was Aisha's strategy, meant to play on both the party's superior numbers and the favorable topography. It all rested on her faith in the highly precise shooting ability of the center guard.

The lambton could no longer even burrow underground. As the front line pressed back the thrashing, writhing monster, the Amazon completed her Concurrent Chant, leaped backward, and threw her *podao* against the ground.

"Hell Kaios!"

The magic, with the full force of Aisha's energy behind it, was released.

The slicing wave imbued with powerful mental force transformed into a four-meder-long guillotine and rushed forward. Unleashed next to the monster's side, the deadly weapon landed directly on the scarlet collar, then kept moving forward.

The lambton perished, unable even to let out a death cry as the blade sliced off its head, magic item and all.

"Yeah!!"

"We beat a deep-level monster!"

"Ouka and I on the front line are pretty beat up...but we did it."

"Ouka! Are you okay?"

"We got some drop items, too!"

"I can't believe how greedy you are, Lilliluka..."

Welf pumped his fist at the splendid defeat of the deep-level monster, and Mikoto grinned as she wiped the blood from her face.

Welf and Ouka were the most beaten-up of the group, having stood throughout as a wall against the lambton's attacks, and their shields were thoroughly battered as well. As Chigusa brought them potions, Lilly cheerfully collected the wormwell's sharp fangs and cranial shell, along with its extremely pure magic stones. Only Daphne looked bored.

Meanwhile, Aisha squinted, as if she was quite proud to have lived up to her reputation, and smiled with relief.

"Lady Cassandra, I threw off my backpack with all my items in it, so would you mind working your recovery magic on everyone? I'm sorry to be so useless..." Haruhime said, ashamed, as she turned to the party's lone healer for help.

"Miss...Cassandra?"

The girl stood rooted in place, as if she hadn't heard a thing.

Was this...the calamity?

She looked out at the members of her party, bubbling with excitement over their victory, and at the monster's corpse, which was already mostly turned to ash.

This is all?

At one point, Cassandra believed that the deep-level monster was the calamity her prophetic dream had warned of, but that belief had been turned upside down.

It wasn't menacing enough.

It wasn't terrifying enough.

It didn't provoke enough despair.

It ended too quickly.

It just didn't seem worthy of the term *catastrophe*.

"This isn't it," she murmured, deciding within herself that this wasn't the actualization of her dream.

To the contrary, if her dream had been no more than this, how relieved she would have been.

But the scenes she had seen in her dream had been far crueler and more ominous. There had been no hope of being saved.

This was not the calamity...!

No. True despair still lay ahead of them.

"Heh-heh-heh...Ha-ha-ha-ha-ha-ha-ha-ha-ha-ha-ha-ha-ha-ha-ha!!"

Laughter spills out of the catman as if his mouth is broken, his armless shoulder jerking up and down. His body is folded over like he's having a fit, and his tail—which is broken off halfway down—dances behind him.

Lyu and I both stare as Jura, who should be cowering in a corner, puts on this ridiculous display.

"You think it's over? You're wrong. This is just the *beginning*!!"

He roars with laughter, tears gathering at the corners of his eyes.

"Do you want to know why I chose this spot for the 'ceremony,' Leon?"

"What are you talking about...?!"

"The Water Capital is linked across this zone! The whole area connected by the Great Falls is like one floor! Damage in one place is shared everywhere! That's what the Dungeon *thinks*, at least!"

Lyu jumps as if she's just been struck by lightning.

Damage? Shared? The Dungeon...thinks?

I seem to be the only one who doesn't get what's going on. The catman's vulgar laugh echoes across the room.

"It doesn't matter if the explosion is on the twenty-fifth floor or the twenty-seventh...To the Dungeon, it's as if the wounds were on the same floor!"

Lyu's expression transforms.

"I even used the magic you released!"

"No way...?!"

"Did you think things would still be okay with this level of damage?"

He grins, and a second later—

Bang!

The ceiling of the room we're in shakes.

"You were chasing me so desperately—but I'm just a decoy!"

Fragments of crystal rain down on us.

There seems to have been an explosion on one of the higher floors, as if to carry on the series of explosions that occurred on this floor.

The twenty-fifth floor is screaming.

"Stop..." Lyu says, looking up at the ceiling as I stand here astonished. "Stop!!"

For the first time, her voice has lost its calm.

She's screaming in panic.

The catman ignores her.

"—Do it, Turk!" he shouts.

"Huff...puff...huff...!!"

As the werewolf ran through the Dungeon, he tore off his companions' backpacks and scattered the bright-red balls within them onto the passageway floors.

Ignoring the monsters chasing after them, the small band of men kept on running and scattering more red balls.

"O-o-okay, here we go...I'm gonna light them now!"

Having dropped all the balls, they dove for shelter and drew their magic blades.

The objects they were looking at were Inferno Stones. Collected as drop items from flame rocks, a type of deep-level monster, they had strong fire-starting power and explosiveness even when used as is.

"Fire!"

Crouching in a twenty-fifth-floor passageway crowded with monsters, Turk and his companions aimed for the red balls and brought down their magic blades.

The flames that shot from their ends spread, and the Inferno Stones glowed.

A moment later, a massive explosion rocked the Dungeon.

"—Ahh!"

The monsters that had been following Turk's band of men were swallowed up in the ball of flames.

It didn't stop there, however.

The Inferno Stones they had scattered haphazardly down the passageways lit up like a fuse, exploding and spreading the flames farther and farther, destroying one passage after the next.

Burning monsters and melted crystal columns alike were swept away in the whirlwind of destruction.

"?!"

"What's happening?!"

The shock waves had reached the spot on the same floor where Aisha, Welf, and the rest of their party were standing.

Meanwhile, two floors below, adventurers looked up as the thundering explosions reached them.

"B-Bors?!"

"What is this? What's going on?!"

Above them, crystal walls were blown away, floors burst open, ceilings collapsed, and waterways overflowed their banks in chaos.

One section of the multilayered twenty-fifth floor collapsed entirely, having lost its supports.

"The ground is collapsing…!!"

"Run! Run!!"

Welf and the rest of his party fled desperately to avoid being sucked down with the collapsing structure.

In the huge cavern, the Great Falls spit out a mass of crystal debris and monster corpses, swelling and roaring like a tidal wave.

The scream of the Dungeon was unending.

* * *

The explosions continue.

As the lights blink and the crystals in the room vibrate and jump up and down from the shocks, the catman stands in front of us laughing.

"I knew you'd chase after me like a madwoman! That's why I'm the decoy! The plan was that once I almost finished destroying the twenty-seventh floor, Turk would take over on the twenty-fifth!"

He's shouting joyfully as crystals fall from the ceiling around him.

"While you were chasing me so frantically, my underlings were setting off the bombs on the other floor. So how does it feel to be set up, eh?"

A chill runs down my spine as the catman roars with laughter again despite what's going on around him. I can't keep up with his logic.

Bombs?

Destroy the twenty-fifth floor?

What are these guys trying to do?

"You didn't pay attention when I threw out those bombs a little while ago, did you? You were careless, weren't you? Isn't that right, Leon? Ha-ha-ha-ha! Caught you, didn't I?"

The next instant, Lyu—who had been staring up at the ceiling in a daze—glares and flies at the catman.

"JURAAAAA!"

She grabs the shirt at his chest and pulls him onto the ground.

"Do you realize what you've done? Do you?!" she shouts.

Her fist trembles, as if she's trying to hold back her emotions.

The catman keeps on smiling despite the blow he's received and doesn't answer her question. Instead, he continues screaming at her.

"Did you think I was just lazing around in these five years since you ruined my life?! No, I was busy researching! Where was the best place to call forth despair? How could I do it?!"

"Huh?"

"The whole time, I was thinking about how I could crush that pretty face of yours!"

"—Aaaaaaaaaaaaah!!"

The distraught Lyu pulls out her dagger and brings it down toward the catman.

But I stop her.

"It's no good, Miss Lyu!"

"Let me go! Let me go!"

All her strength is directed toward pulling out of my full nelson.

The catman slowly stands up, giggling through his teeth.

What is happening?

We were supposed to have him backed into a corner, but now we're the ones who are trapped!

As that thought crosses my mind—

"?!"

The strongest explosion yet rocks us like some kind of grand finale. And then—

The Dungeon *wails*.

"—"

It's not the cracking sound the Dungeon makes when a monster is being born.

It's not the quaking that comes before an irregularity occurs.

It is literally a wail.

A violent, inorganic, high-pitched keening.

It's like a knife being drawn across a taut silver bowstring, piercing my eardrums.

Or a soprano the size of the whole world crying out.

This violent, unmistakable wail of the Dungeon sets my instincts flashing red.

"Aaah…Aaaaah…!"

I can't block my ears, since I'm still restraining Lyu, but my whole body is tense. Just then, the strength drains from her body.

"It's just like that time…all over again…Aaah, Alize…!"

"Miss Lyu? Miss Lyu?"

Her slim body collapses, and I scramble to support her. I'm calling her name in a panic as her face turns white and then blue.

I don't know this Lyu.

Who is this person with the vacant eyes hollowed out by trauma?

"Run…Escape!!"

"What…?"

She looks up at me as she utters her command in a broken voice.

Our faces are so close they're nearly touching. She's gripping my clothes.

"Get out of here as fast as you can!! Even if you have to go alone—hurry!!"

That's when I understand.

Now it makes sense why she tried so hard to get rid of me when I first encountered her on this floor.

She was afraid something like this was going to happen.

The catman stands up.

"It's too late!" he howls.

He looks up at the ceiling as if he's pointing with his missing arm.

"You and I, we're both trapped in despair!"

His smile twitches. He, too, is pale.

"Come and get us! Show yourself!" he shouts, like he's throwing down his chips on the gamble of his life. His voice is full of joy.

"Appear before us once again!!"

"—"

The prophetess of tragedy lowered one knee to the ground.

"Cassandra?"

"Lady Cassandra?"

She could not hear Daphne's voice. She could not see Haruhime or the others who ran to her side. Flashes of light were running through her head. She knew "that time" had come.

"Aa…Aaa…"

The wails of the Dungeon were the "lament."

Her face was as pale as Lyu's. She grabbed her head with both hands, frozen in place as the prophecy fell from her lips.

"'A great calamity…draws near.'"

Crack!

A fissure spread through the cavern on the twenty-seventh floor.

It was a long, wide, deep fissure, running vertically opposite the Great Falls.

The first thing to spring from the fissure was liquid.

The purple serum spewed out like blood, steam rising from it. The emerald-blue water clouded as if it had been soiled with sewer sludge.

The crack widened, scattering fragments of crystal, as if the Dungeon were splitting open its own womb.

Finally.

A scarlet eye glinted from the depths of the fissure.

Despair let out its newborn cry.

CHAPTER 5

CALAMITY ARRIVES

"Bors, this is bad!"

"I've never heard the Dungeon make this noise before! Let's get outta here!"

The adventurers had gathered together again after being scattered by their encounter with Gale Wind, and they were now chasing her and Bell in a group.

They were determined to kill the legendary fugitive with their own hands. She had managed to get away after the surprise attack, but they were sure that with a group this big, they would be able to take her down.

Things were changing quickly, however.

There had been the tremendous explosions on the twenty-fifth floor, and now the wails that were unquestionably coming from the Dungeon. Everyone guessed that the high-frequency sounds, so loud they could not stand to leave their ears uncovered, signaled an irregularity.

The upper-class adventurers knew something unprecedented was about to happen, and without exception they petitioned the head of Rivira to evacuate the party from the floor.

"Hey, Bors! Bors!"

"...Wait."

"Huh?"

They stopped moving as Bors thrust his palm toward them.

He removed his other hand from the side of his giant eye-patch-adorned head and muttered.

"The sound...has stopped."

The mermaid wrapped her arms around her body.

Ugh...I hate this sound...!

She was deep underwater, surrounded by bluish darkness.

She had dived down to escape the horrible cry of her mother, the Dungeon, trying to hide in the water. Her body curled like a fetus, she desperately pressed her hands against the fins that served as her ears.

I'm scared, scared, scared...!

It had happened before, just once.

It had been five years ago, she was sure.

She had heard her mother's lament coming from far deeper in the Dungeon. Of course, that time it had nothing to do with Mari, who could not leave the Water Capital, but still, she had been frightened.

Something bad had been born that time, too. She didn't know much, but she knew that. She understood.

Mari pressed her hands to her ears and squeezed her eyes shut.

She had escaped to the depths of the water in an attempt to separate herself from the terrifying reality. But behind her shut eyelids, she saw her friends and her family—the Xenos.

The Xenos, and an image of the back of the boy she had met so recently in the Dungeon.

That boy, who was as important to her as her own family, was here.

He was already among her most prized treasures.

Bell...!

She pushed away her fear and forced her eyes open.

Her tears spilling into the water and her tail beating against it, the mermaid swam toward the surface where the light filtered in.

"That was close..." Lilly muttered, ignoring the bead of sweat that was dripping down her chin.

Before her eyes was a collapsed crystal floor. Far below, she could see the raging waterway.

Her party had barely managed to escape disaster thus far as they ran through the crumbling twenty-fifth floor, explosions ringing out all around them and destroying anything resembling a road.

They didn't know how extensive the damage was, but they knew it was bad. In any case, it was no time to be fighting monsters, who were in the same situation as they were.

The water paradise had become a ruined capital, and some routes were now impassable. Lilly feared that until the Dungeon finished repairing itself, they would not be able to make it back to the passageway that led to the twenty-fourth floor.

"I'm worried about these explosions, but…!"

"That insanely high-pitched noise just a minute ago…Was that from the twenty-seventh floor?!"

"If that was an irregularity, then Sir Bell…?!"

Aisha, Welf, and Mikoto were equally distraught.

"Cassandra! Cassandra! Pull yourself together!"

"Lady Cassandra?"

But the healer was more upset than any of them.

She was collapsed on the floor, unresponsive to Daphne, who was kneeling by her side and shaking her shoulder, or Haruhime, who was frantically calling her name.

The strength had drained from her legs, and she gripped her head in both hands. Her face was white. Her blood had drained away to the point that her companions wondered whether it was possible for a person to sink that deeply into despair.

It was strange.

Lilly couldn't understand what had happened.

Ouka and Welf felt the same as they looked on, holding their breath nervously.

Their ability to think was dulled in the midst of the chaos.

Lilly could barely make out what Cassandra was saying.

"…n…un…"

She was shrieking something over and over.

"Run…!"

As the sound of shattering crystal rocks rang out, *it* silently appeared from within the fissure.

Spawned from the wall of the cavern, it fell into the plunge pool with a tremendous splash.

Its newborn cry was an unpleasantly warm sigh.

As the crashing sound of the Great Falls beat against its skin, the white mist veiled its silhouette.

It neither howled nor roared a battle cry but instead swished its long tail and moved its two legs, sending ripples across the water's surface.

Deep in its eye socket, a sinister crimson light glinted.

At the edge of the plunge pool as broad as a lake, it bent its joints, and its knees creaked.

The next instant, *it disappeared.*

It had burst from the water's surface and into the floor's internal maze.

"Hey, shouldn't we try to meet up with Bors?"

"Idiot. We save our own skins first!"

The small band of adventurers was on the twenty-seventh floor, but they had been unable to meet up with Bors's main party. Instead, the four-man party comprised of humans and animal people had hurriedly turned back up the road they came down. They had lost their nerve in the face of the Dungeon's irregularity.

For a bunch of hooligans who made their living by exploring the Dungeon, it was the obvious course of action.

But things didn't go as they expected.

"...? What's that noise...?"

Bam-bam-bam-bam-bam!

A strange sound was coming from behind them.

It sounded like something was jumping up and down. The adventurers stopped and looked over their shoulders.

The noise was quickly approaching them.

A shadow flickered in the depths of the passage.

"Huh?"

"Something's com—"

Pop!

There was a rather pleasant sound, and then the adventurer's head burst open, so that he could not finish his sentence.

Even when his final moment came, he did not know what had happened.

He had become a silent lump of flesh, with fountains of blood spurting from him as his knees sank to the ground.

It happened four times.

They were annihilated.

It ignored the fresh blood dripping from its claws and trampled on the adventurers' corpses.

As its massive shadow fell over the maze, the monster reversed course.

It was headed toward its next prey.

"A...Aaaaaaaaaaaaaaaaaaaaaaaaaaaaaaaaaaaaaaaaaaaa aaaaa!!"

A scream echoed through the Dungeon.

It was the wail of a weeping lancer.

His small party had been demolished by a sudden attack.

The elven sorcerer had been killed first. She had been determined to purge her shameful fellow elf Gale Wind from their race, and her pridefulness verged on bragging, making her an unpleasant woman to be around. Still, although she was not docile, she was thoughtful in her strange way, and he had thought her something of a good woman. She was the first to fall victim to the claws. Her body was ripped in half at the waist. Her guts spilled out and blood dripped from her vacant eyes. She had died in a way no proud elf would willingly allow. And so the man had lost control of himself and thrust his sword forward. But it met only air. Everything before him went black, and his head split open.

When he fell, his hand brushed the cheek of the elf who cried tears of blood.

"What is this thing? I don't know...What are youuuuuuuu?!"

The fifth adventurer, a half elf and the last one left standing, pulled out his magic blade.

There was an explosion followed by flames.

When the smoke cleared, *it* had disappeared, leaving *the burned corpse of the fifth adventurer* sprawled in the passage.

* * *

The shadow ran and danced, and then the next one did, and the next.

The Dungeon filled with screams.

Screams of agony were joined by fountains of blood.

“Aaaaaaaaaaaaaaaaaaaaaaaaaaaaaaaaaaaaaaaaaaaaaaaaaa aaaaaaaaaaaaaaaaaaaaaaaaaaaaaaaaaaaaaaaaaaaaaaaaaaa!!”

Faster and faster, so fast it was unbelievable, the corpses multiplied.

It had a merciless sense of where the adventurers were, and it snuffed out their lives one by one.

Its slashing claws tore apart whatever they came in contact with. Its biting fangs chewed through flesh and armor alike. Its thrashing tail knocked blood from the mouths of adventurers.

There was nothing the fifty-some adventurers on the twenty-seventh floor could do. They were simply slaughtered.

“Noooooooooooooooooooooooooooooooooooooooooooo ooooooooo!!”

All who saw it cried out.

“What is that huge thi—?!”

All who saw it trembled with fear.

“The t-t-t-t-t-t-t-t-t-t t-t-t-t-t-t-t-t-t-t-t-t-t-t-t-t-t-t-t-t t-t-t-t-teeth are…”

All who saw it were destroyed and devoured.

Their screams echoed.

Their weapons shattered.

They tried to run, but they could not.

“Bors, save us!! Sav—Aaah!!”

“Eeeeeeeeeeeeeeeeeeeeeeeeeeeeeeeeeeeeeeeeeeeeeeeeeee eee!!”

The banquet was unending.

There were many “wails” as the “road of viscera” was built within the crystal maze.

The “azure current” now “ran red with blood.”

As the corpses of the adventurers multiplied one by one, the monsters—the "grotesque horde"—rejoiced.

They drank the blood of the humans that stained the waterways as if it were fresh dew, and they greedily devoured the bodies the water carried to them as if they were the finest meat.

Some adventurers bloomed into "flowers of flesh."

Some were "swiftly torn asunder."

Some were "shattered."

The dignity of some became as "playthings."

Those who tried in desperation to escape were knocked down by other monsters, who swarmed around them and tore them apart with "countless fangs and claws," and they were "mourned" all the more miserably.

Those who died and left their comrades behind "imparted sorrow." But those who mourned them soon followed the same path.

The Water Capital had transformed into the stage for a massacre.

"Oh my…!"

"This is…"

When they saw it, Chigusa trembled in fear and Ouka was stunned.

They were in the cavern on the twenty-fifth floor.

Lilly and the rest of the party stood on the cliff at the mouth of the waterfall, near the passage leading to the twenty-sixth floor, and looked down on the scene as the falling water thundered in their ears. They had just emerged into the cavern.

The Great Falls ran red. A faint, fleeting red.

The cascade, which was directly connected to the waterways within the maze, was spitting out a river of blood produced by the monsters' feast. The emerald-blue of the plunge pool on the twenty-seventh floor was but a faint memory.

Bobbing in the water far below, so distant they looked to Lilly and the others like black specks, were the dismembered legs and arms of the half-devoured corpses. The pitiful fragments of weapons and adventurers floated and sank at the lowest level of the water paradise.

The "depths of hell" overflowed with corpses, returning all to the "mother," the Dungeon.

"No way…Is that all…blood…?"

Welf could not conceal the shaking in his voice.

"It's insane; how many adventurers…? Not *everyone* who went to the twenty-seventh floor…?"

Mikoto's voice, too, faded away as she contemplated the possibility.

"Please stop joking around!! Mr. Bell is still alive! Mr. Bell is…!" Lilly said in a panic.

Haruhime, even more panicked than Lilly, had gone completely white.

"Ah, aaah…!!"

Even Aisha was in a daze.

"…What the hell is happening?"

The second-tier adventurer shifted her gaze from the bloodred plunge pool to the fissure opposite it.

For a moment, she forgot to breathe as she imagined what had been spawned from that all-too-deep crevice.

"…Let's go to the twenty-seventh floor! I don't know what's happening, but we have to save Mr. Bell!" Lilly shouted. Far above her, standing on the cliff by the passage leading to the twenty-fourth floor, another group of adventurers was screaming.

The tunnel leading to the inside of the twenty-sixth floor was on the southeastern side of the cavern where Lilly and the others stood now. For *Hestia Familia*, the floors below were an unknown world, but all nodded back at Lilly. Neither Welf nor Mikoto nor Haruhime hesitated for even an instant.

Lilly was about to take off running through the cavern with the others in tow when Cassandra, who had been silent up to that point, grabbed her hand.

"!! Miss Cassandra! This isn't the time to play arou—"

She broke off mid-word when she looked up at the face of the girl grasping her small hand in both of her own.

"Cassan…dra…?" Daphne said, standing as still as Lilly.

Welf and the others had stopped as well and were staring silently at Cassandra.

"I'm sorry…I'm sorry; I'm sorry; I'm sorry…!"

She was sobbing, but she would not let go of Lilly's hand.

Her face was filled with despair. She hung her head as tears overflowed from her eyes. She was apologizing to those who were not there.

"I'm sorry; I'm sorry…!!"

She was apologizing to the countless adventurers she had given up on because they would not believe her.

And also to the boy she had allowed to go to the place of disaster.

She could not stop apologizing.

This was the "banquet of calamity."

The Dungeon said nothing. It merely accepted the blood that flew onto its walls, as if this was the proper course of events. The crystals that had sparkled blue before were stained with blood now, transforming the fantastical scene that had struck Bell's party with wonder into a picture of hell.

The Dungeon knew how their journey would end.

No one would return alive.

The crystals on the ceiling have dimmed now, like magic-stone lanterns about to run out of energy, because of the explosions on the twenty-fifth floor. As the room grows ever darker, sounds reach our ears.

"This is…?!"

The chaotic howls of monsters.

The sound of *something* shaking the Dungeon.

And mixed in with it all, distant but distinctly human screams.

The sounds intertwine in a strange, unsettling melody.

What are these sounds?

What are these screams?!

As I support Lyu's body, I cannot prevent myself from screaming at the man in front of us.

"What did you do?!"

"It's a ceremony, you see!"

He smiles with deep joy.

"A ceremony to wake me from my nightmare!"

"Nightmare...?"

His sunken eyes shine glassily, as if he's gone mad.

It's hopeless. I have no idea what he's talking about.

What spurs on my panic is the fact that this guy standing in front of us grinning is in just as bad a situation as we are. He's dripping sweat as monsters keep howling and the Dungeon shakes, and he looks like his teeth are about to start chattering.

As if he, too, is heading toward the jaws of death—.

But what worries me even more than that is the way Lyu—who's always been so calm and cool—is acting right now.

"Jura...!"

She steps away from my arms and tries to calm her ragged breath. But her small frame will not obey her will. As if she is battling a fear on the verge of overflowing or, more likely, because she cannot escape the chains of trauma that bind her, she continues to shake violently.

She wraps her arms tightly around her chest and glares piercingly at the catman. Far from shrinking, however, he seems to find the situation enjoyable.

"So you still haven't figured it out, eh, Rabbit Foot, even though Leon is so upset she's practically dying?" He jeers at me. "I've called it here to the twenty-seventh floor!"

"Stop!!"

He ignores Lyu's plea and merely shouts again. His next words leave me speechless.

"I've summoned the beast that butchered *Astrea Familia*!"

"!!"

Ouranos rose from his throne.

"Ouranos, what's wrong?"

He was in the Chamber of Prayers beneath the Guild, a stone room reminiscent of a temple. Four torches set on the altar of the underground room threw off a red glow. Standing in the center of the shadowy space, the god widened his blue eyes.

Even via the oculus, Fels sensed the gravity of a situation that prompted the aged deity to rise from his chair. Under ordinary circumstances, he scarcely moved.

For Ouranos, time stood still. He spoke gravely.

"That thing has come out…"

"Thing? What are you referring to? What are you saying, Ouranos?"

Fels's voice rose in panic in response to the god's strange behavior.

Ouranos gazed through narrowed eyes toward the underground world spread beneath his feet as he spoke into the crystal ball.

"The monster that decimated *Astrea Familia* five years ago…"

"…?!"

Ouranos continued to speak solemnly to the dumbstruck Fels.

"The calamity has begun again…"

"Five years ago, my familia, *Rudra Familia*, was in a feud with *Astrea Familia*, you see! I don't know who was in the right or whatever, but they were getting in the way of us Evils and we couldn't stand it! So we decided to trap them in the Dungeon!"

Bell gaped in shock as Jura's words echoed through the room on the twenty-seventh floor.

A signal throbbed in the back of his mind.

What he was hearing now was linked to the story Lyu had told him on the eighteenth floor.

"Just like today, we collected a whole lot of fire bombs! We thought we'd lure Leon and her familia down there and bury them alive! But those tough bastards didn't die. We actually ended up on the defensive!"

Fear and anger rose in Jura's eyes as he recalled that day. Suddenly, though, his emotions seemed to cool, and an unsettling smile curled his lips.

"But then...something happened that we hadn't expected."

Lyu's face distorted, and Jura flinched.

"Unexpected...?" Bell asked, sweat dripping down his face.

The catman went pale, but all the same, he continued to grin.

"A monster spawned from the Dungeon, you see."

"When excessive damage occurs, it provokes a self-protective instinct...The Dungeon's lament was so terrible even my prayers could not reach it."

Ouranos spoke sorrowfully as he listened to the continuing voice of the Dungeon.

On that day five years ago, *Rudra Familia* had recklessly brought masses of Inferno Stones into the Dungeon, causing huge explosions to erupt on one of the floors.

The damage had been so extensive the term *maze* no longer held any meaning.

And then the Dungeon had sent out its warning signal.

"If they had simply damaged the structure of the maze, nothing much would have happened. The Dungeon would have repaired itself and regenerated. It has such great power that the children call it an 'infinite resource'..."

"But if destructive behavior is so great, so excessive...that the regeneration cannot keep pace..."

"Yes...The Dungeon chooses not regeneration but elimination of the source of the damage."

It was quite simple, really, if one thought of the Dungeon as a living creature.

When a foreign organism attacks a human internally, the immune system acts to kill the invading pathogen. This is the natural self-defensive instinct of all living creatures.

The same holds true for the Dungeon.

As the adventurers say, "The Dungeon is alive."

When the womb of all monsters is attacked too fiercely, the living underground maze activates its defensive instincts and spawns a being that serves as its immune response.

This being that kills foreign organisms—in this case, invading adventurers—can be thought of as the Dungeon's apostle. And it shakes off even the will of Ouranos, whose role is to hold the Dungeon in check.

"Are you saying that the same level of damage that occurred five years ago has happened once again?" Fels asked.

"That seems to be the case..."

The being the Dungeon spawned five years ago was an Irregular.

Ouranos had not anticipated it, meaning neither had *Astrea Familia* or *Rudra Familia*; it was a truly unknown monster.

Loki Familia had never seen it, nor had *Freya Familia*, nor had either of the two largest familias at the time, those of Zeus and Hera. Which is to say, in the thousand years since the deities had descended to the mortal plane, the phenomenon had been observed only once.

Only Ouranos, who prayed to the Dungeon for mercy, had noticed it.

And only the victims of this nameless monster had ever laid eyes upon it.

"Except for me, everyone was killed! That shitty woman from *Astrea Familia* and me!"

As Bell listened to the full story that Lyu had kept from him, everything but shock drained from his mind.

Beside him, Lyu's face was filled with pain.

"For the past five years, I've been looking into what happened! I investigated all the details of what caused it and how I could summon that monster again! I didn't ask any of the Evils' Remnants—I did it all myself!"

Bell could not believe his ears as he listened to Jura's overheated explanation. His head still swimming with astonishment and his lips trembling, he finally spoke.

"Why? Why did you want to summon that thing again...?"

"So I could train it, obviously!!" Jura snapped back instantly. "Even though I was pissing and shitting myself that time, as a tamer I couldn't take my eyes off it. Leon, did it look like a monster to you? Not to me! To me, it was more beautiful than a goddess!!"

Lyu returned Jura's glance with an indecipherable gaze.

For the first time, the catman's voice was trembling.

A monster lover.

The phrase rose to Bell's mind.

"Its presence was overwhelming, killing everything, destroying everything! I wanted it; I wanted it all for myself!!"

Perhaps because he was a tamer, his eyes glittered like a child's, and his voice throbbed with a perverse joy.

At the time, even though the overwhelming awe and fear had made his whole body tremble, he had earnestly longed to possess the monster. Jura had, in a sense, deified and worshipped the horrible creature.

In other words, the one-armed tamer had been enraptured by the beast whose overwhelming power gave rise to such tragedy.

Lyu glared angrily at Jura as he revealed his deepest motivations.

"Idiot! That monster is different! It's not like that! It's not something that can be tamed!"

"Not by ordinary methods! But I have this!!"

Jura pulled out an expandable collar. By resonating with the whip, the magic item fashioned by the Evils could tame even monsters from the deep levels.

"And with it here, I'm not afraid of anything!! I cannot be threatened!"

"...?!"

"Not even by you, Leon!"

Jura pointed at Lyu with his remaining hand, his loathing burning high.

"Until now, there hasn't been a single night when you didn't haunt my dreams! Yes, they were nightmares! But when I summon that monster...Yes! I will overcome the nightmare of that day!"

As Bell listened to the furious stream of words, the meaning of *nightmare* and *overcome* were clear to him. Lyu was the embodiment of Jura's trauma, and he planned to use her personal trauma to humiliate and erase her.

There was no room for sympathy toward this man.

All the same, Bell could see that he, too, was another individual tormented by the past.

"It's mine! I'll never give it up!" he howled, looking toward the ceiling.

Five years of investigation and research had led Jura to two conclusions.

First, no matter how much damage was inflicted on the upper levels, the Dungeon would not let out its "wail," or even so much as a warning. This was because the zone near the surface was heavily affected by the will of Ouranos. Therefore, he determined, the monster could not be summoned to that area.

His second conclusion had to do with the conditions needed for the nameless monster to appear. The damage to the floors had to be *so severe*, the Dungeon could not keep up with repairs. If that level of damage was inflicted, the monster would be spawned on the same floor. The monster could not be summoned without taking certain measures. By comparing the number of Inferno Stones his familia used five years ago and the data on damage to the Dungeon against hundreds of locations on maps, Jura had determined that approximately 20 percent of a given floor had to be destroyed. In other words, the very structure of the Dungeon had to be undermined.

Jura had tamed and then sacrificed a large number of monsters during his five years of experiments in destruction. Based on the minute reactions of the Dungeon, he had finally concluded that the Dungeon viewed the entire Water Capital as a single floor.

"No one knew of this Dungeon taboo. If we had issued some sort of regulation, we would have ended up revealing that something was there...So we had no choice but to keep quiet and suppress the truth," Ouranos said.

The assumption was that under ordinary circumstances, no one would be able to cause large-scale damage to the sprawling floors of the middle levels or below. Who, after all, would risk their own life to do such a thing?

Astrea Familia, which had witnessed the monster, had been wiped out, and *Rudra Familia* had been exterminated to the last man by Gale Wind.

Lyu was the only one left who knew the truth about what had happened, and Ouranos had not thought that she—having experienced tragedy so directly—would ever test the limits of the taboo.

In other words, *it* should never have spawned again.

That would have been true, if Gale Wind had not failed to kill Jura.

"I revealed everything to the Xenos. They sensed the Irregular five years ago and were terrified of it. I sought their help in ensuring such a thing would never happen again. But..."

"Right now, Lido and the other Xenos are participating in the invasion of Knossos...!" Fels groaned, the blinking crystals illuminating the mage's face through the oculus.

Ouranos nodded gravely.

"Yes. There is no way to respond swiftly to the situation."

"And it's happening in the middle—no, the lower levels...Just where the expedition headed...It can't be! *Hestia Familia* is down there?"

"Taming a monster...? A monster so horrible it wiped out Lyu's whole familia...And you called it to this floor?"

Bell could not piece together all the information that had been thrown at him so quickly.

It's no use! I can't keep up.

As the sound of his own heart pounded unpleasantly in his ears, Bell frantically tried to understand.

So the monster that Jura intentionally called here by destroying the floors is Lyu's true enemy...

That nightmare was never supposed to return.

But now it was rampaging through this floor, exterminating what it viewed as a virus. In other words—

"—Bors?!"

Having finally figured out what was going on, Bell turned toward the entrance of the room and the maze beyond, where he could still hear monsters howling as if in celebration.

The faces of the adventurers in Bors's party rose before his mind's eye, and he was about to take off running in their direction when Lyu grabbed his arm.

"Miss Lyu?!"

"No…!"

Her delicate elf's hand was as white as snow.

"You must not go! If you try to fight that thing…!"

For the first time, Bell saw a look of pleading fill her face. Her normally resolute blue eyes wavered with despair. It was as if she was crying without any tears—as if she was looking through him and pleading with some phantom of the past not to go forward.

Bell was torn over what to do. He said nothing.

"That's right, Leon! You can't let it go, can you?! You fought that monster yourself, and you know even better than I do how terrifying it is!"

Once again, Jura cackled.

"Not to mention…"

Bell gasped at the catman's next words.

"…the fact that you don't want to butcher more of your friends with your own hands!"

Lyu's face seemed to crack.

"Oh yes, that's what you did!"

"Shut up."

"To save your precious self!"

"Shut up!"

"*By sacrificing your friends*, you were finally able to drive off the monster!"

"Shut uuuuuuuuuuuuuuuup!!"

The catman laughed.

Bell stood rooted to the ground.

Lyu threw her head back and howled.

The three of them were trapped in the chaos of their entangled emotions.

Just at that instant, a roar thundered through the Dungeon.

For a moment, after the hair-raising roar died down, the entire floor was silent.

Bell couldn't breathe. Lyu stood frozen. Jura shuddered.

Both the carefully cultivated senses of the three adventurers and their most basic animal instincts were screaming warning signals.

The tremor of horror lasted for only a second.

The floor quaked in unison, and when the momentary hush was shattered, a mad rush of men and women flooded into the room where Bell stood.

"Aaaaaaaaaaaaaaaaaaaaaaaaaaaaaaaaaaaaaaah!!"

The pack of adventurers arrived with Bors at the head.

It was the hunting party that both Bell and Lyu knew so well.

Only now, its size had clearly shrunk.

Those who remained were spattered with copious amounts of blood—and it was not their own.

Bell gaped at them.

"Mr. Bor—"

His scream died mid-word.

A pair of bloodred eyes floated faintly in the darkness beyond the entrance to the room. Icy claws gripped his heart.

...There it is.

An instant later, the shadow disappeared into the darkness.

"—"

Bell heard the sound of crystal being crushed underfoot, and then a flash of movement grazed past Bors and his party as they tried to

© Suzuhito Yasud

flee. It continued on without stopping, whizzing at a slant over Bell's head.

He didn't even have a chance to react.

By the time he whipped his head around, one member of Bors's party was missing.

Gripped by terror, still not understanding what had happened, he scanned the room behind him.

Nothing was there.

"Aa…Aaaa…"

It was above him.

Like a giant spider, it clung there gripping the joint between the wall and the ceiling.

The ill-fated missing adventurer was clenched between its jaws.

"—"

The form illuminated by the light of the crystals was huge and thin.

It had two arms and two legs. The long, thin arms were bizarrely out of proportion with the body. The legs, too, were long and thin but bent backward at the joints. Oddly, the bony, nearly fleshless form was covered in a shell that at first glance looked like a coat of armor. It glinted with a strange dark-purplish-blue light. From the base of its back extended a hard four-meder-long tail.

Its bumpy head was identical to a beast's skull, except for the crimson light that glowed within the two empty eye sockets. The color was deeper and far more malicious than that of Bell's rubellite eyes.

If Bell had to describe the monster's overall appearance, he would have called it a "dinosaur fossil wearing armor."

Even among the innumerable monsters inhabiting the Dungeon, it was clearly an Irregular.

"—"

Its body, suspended upside down as it gripped the crystal wall with the claws of its feet and stared down at Bell and the other adventurers, measured three meders long. There was no question this was a large-category monster.

Its most conspicuous feature was its fang-like claws. Extending from the ends of its bony six-fingered hands, the disproportionately long claws glittered deep purple. At the sight of them, Lyu sank into despair and Jura smiled twitchily.

The monster that inflicted such tragedy five years ago had appeared once again before the two adventurers, and now for the first time, Bell was seeing it, too.

Its crimson eyes scrutinized the remaining adventurers.

"H-help m—"

Crunch.

Before the eyes of the stunned Bell, the monster bit through the adventurer it held between its teeth, as if doing so was the most ordinary thing in the world.

Here was the prime culprit behind *Astrea Familia*'s suffering.

At the time, people had said it would only be a matter of time before the young female adventurers who made up the familia attained first-tier status. But this one monster had decimated them, erasing their future in a matter of minutes.

Two had been Level Three. Eight had been Level Four.

This nameless monster had wiped out all ten of these second-tier adventurers.

Although the Guild's records made no mention of the beast, Ouranos had bestowed a name upon it.

Juggernaut.

The destroyer.

The adventurer's head quietly fell from between the monster's fangs and split open on the ground.

Bors and the others went pale as they watched. Bell's mind went blank.

The monster moved again.

"—"

Its knees bent backward, extended—and once again it vanished.

"—?!"

It moved with unbelievable speed.

The wind it threw off was so strong it blew back the adventurers' hair.

Bell dodged the streak of purple just in the nick of time.

A second later, someone screamed.

"Gyaaaaaaaaaaaaaaaaaaaaaaaaaaaaaaaaaaaaaaaaaaaaaaaaaa!!"

An animal person had been torn into several pieces.

The claws, moving so fast they left behind a deep-purple arc, had murdered him.

It had taken only a single swipe.

The massacre continued unabated.

The beast pulverized a pair of dwarves with its long flail-like tail. They collapsed, vomiting blood. Then it brought down its hand onto an elf, crushing her into the ground. Still gripped within its hand, she fell prey to the fang-like claws. Her arms and legs dropped away from her body, now no more than a mangled lump of meat.

It devoured a human from the head down.

Within a window of time so brief that Bell's mind could not keep up, a chain of five deaths had taken place.

"*Yaaaaaaaaaaaaaaaaaaaa!*"

Half-crazy with fear and anger, the three adventurers in the front guard rushed forward, swinging their greatsword, mace, and battle-ax.

The instant before the weapons landed on their target, the monster crouched nimbly on its backward-bent legs, crushing the crystal floor beneath it, and leaped to the side. The three weapons met nothing but air. The Juggernaut landed beside a huge cluster of crystals, sending up a spray of debris.

It dashed forward again, and the upper bodies of the three adventurers flew into the air.

The purple-blue form did not stop.

Springing *from one crystal column to the next*, it began its mad dance of death.

"Aaaaaah!!"

Each time it passed, fresh blood spewed from adventurers and shredded armor flew toward the ceiling. Like a spider weaving its web, the monster surrounded Bors and his party with intersecting flashes of purple. Caught in this web, the prey vomited blood, lost limbs, and fell to the ground one after the next.

The calamity Cassandra had foreseen in her dream was made real.

What allowed the monster to carry out this slaughter that not even a floor boss could have managed was its ability to *move at super-high speed*. Normally, large-category monsters could not move this fast.

Using the insane power of its legs, it sped like a missile from one corner of the fifty-meder-wide room to the other, efficiently wiping out the virus—that is, the adventurers. It ricocheted off the floor, ceiling, and walls in a continuous series of leaps, swiftly and cruelly massacring the large group of adventurers who had gathered in that chamber of death. They didn't even have time to understand what was happening.

As she watched her nightmare rise to life once again, Lyu's voice caught in her throat.

Even Jura, who was the originator of all the horror, found his legs shaking beneath him.

Bell stared in disbelief.

Adventurers collapsed.

Brave warriors were torn to pieces along with their shields.

Cowards were pierced through as they tried to flee.

The wavering chants of sorcerers turned to requiems as they were murdered.

The rampage wasn't even a battle.

The spectacle of so many deaths in such a brief period of time defied the limits of emotion. As Bell watched the merciless slaughter unfold, he felt neither terror nor despair; instead, it was as if he had been cut loose from all feelings.

"—!!"

Suddenly, he exploded.

With eyes wide open and a wordless roar on his lips, he leaped into the midst of the massacre.

"Mr. Cranell?!"

Perhaps it was fortunate that Bell had not ventured out into the maze and witnessed the deaths of the other adventurers. After all, just the deaths inside the room had been enough to make him lose his cool entirely.

Ignoring Lyu's shout, he accelerated.

"Uaaaaaaaaaaaaaaaaaaaaaaaaaaaaaaaaaaaaaaaaaaaaaaaaaaaaaaaaaaaaaaaaaaaaaaaaaaaaaaaaaaaaaaaaaaa!!"

The savage claws and fangs bore down on the adventurers who not long before had made up Bell's party—the animal-person siblings, the powerful Amazon, and the ax-wielding Bors.

You think I'll let you get away with that?!

Channeling his raging emotions into a roar, Bell scooped up a greatsword that had been dropped by its original owner and charged toward the speeding purple blur.

"!!"

The sword resonated with a low bovine *clang*.

Purplish-blue fragments scattered onto the ground.

The light within the Juggernaut's eye sockets focused in on the boy. It had suffered a direct blow to the side, which forced it to abort its attack. Bell's rubellite eyes had perfectly tracked the high-speed movements of its huge body and responded with an equally accelerated sword blow, which the monster had blocked with one of its long, bony forearms.

"Rabbit Foot?!"

Drenched in blood and sobbing, Bors and his three companions cried out in joy as the Juggernaut stopped in its tracks. For the first time, the unstoppable torrent of violence was momentarily stalled.

© Suzuhito Yasuda

Bell's gaze met the glow of the monster's eye sockets.

In those brief few seconds, he sensed the unfathomable depth of his enemy's skill, and he shuddered.

For its part, the monster recognized the creature in front of it as a menace, and it automatically shifted its priorities so that Bell was now at the top.

Each saw only the other.

The fight to the death between adventurer and monster began.

"Aaaaaa!!"

"!!"

The boy swung his greatsword, and the monster swiped its left forearm.

The whining metal sent fragments of the enemy's armored shell flying into the air. Bell staggered from the Juggernaut's brute strength, yet even as he dripped sweat at the thought of its overwhelming force, he had discovered a point of attack.

Its defenses are weak!

His opponent's shell had cracked under a single blow, and a faint fissure had run down its thin arm.

An instant of battle was enough for Bell to understand. To the extent that the monster's strength and speed had evolved far beyond ordinary limits, its endurance in the face of attack had declined.

Whoever struck first would win!

Having reached this simple, clear conclusion regarding the conditions for victory, Bell spurred his body to even more energetic movement.

"Yah!"

Using the energy from the foot he planted on the ground, he abruptly twisted his upper body to deliver a fierce spinning blow with the greatsword.

The arc of the black scarf around his neck mirrored that of the silver blade.

"——"

In response, the Juggernaut's reverse joints creaked, and it sprang forward.

"Huh?!"

The blow Bell had delivered with all his strength met thin air, and for a moment his enemy vanished from view. He looked up as he heard it *land above him.*

The Juggernaut was suspended upside down from the ceiling.

No way!

Could it really have leaped twenty meders upward in a single bound?

Nope, no way.

There's no way something like this can exist.

On the one hand, it was an insane large-category monster strong enough to kill an upper-class adventurer with a single blow, but on the other, it had the unparalleled speed and agility to easily dodge its opponent's attacks.

Everything Bell thought he knew about monsters was being turned upside down. Still, the knowledge and experience he'd gained so far gave him parallels to work with.

This thing is like a floor boss that moves faster than an iguaçu!

You've gotta be kidding me. What is this? I can't win. It's impossible. I've gotta get out of here.

Bell pushed away the thoughts blaring inside his head, rejecting what both logic and instinct told him.

There's no way I could escape anyway.

He pushed down the fear and unease surging inside him with a ferocious determination to fight, gritting his teeth with an iron will.

"!"

The Juggernaut exhaled a hot breath, fixed its glowing orbs on Bell, and launched itself off the ceiling with a powerful kick.

"Whoa!"

Bell dodged by a hairbreadth the massive arrow of destruction that came hurtling toward him.

The shock waves followed fast and furious. Adventurers who had been standing rooted to the spot were blown backward as the ground burst open to form a crater. Crystal fragments bombarded Bell like scattershot.

The greatsword—which he had pulled aside just a moment too late—was half-demolished.

"What the…?!"

Bell skidded across the ground, tossed aside the greatsword, and thrust out his left hand.

No matter how fast the enemy was, Bell figured it would be no match for the speed of his electrifying flames now that he'd leveled up. He'd use his Swift-Strike Magic to break through the monster's vulnerable defenses.

"It won't work!!"

Lyu's all-out scream came just as Bell opened his own mouth.

"Firebolt!"

Electrical fire spouted from his fist.

The instant before the scarlet lightning bolt exploded into its target, however, the purplish-blue shell encasing the silent Juggernaut pulsed with light.

Instantly, electrifying flames exploded into *Bell's own body.*

"Owww—!"

He stumbled backward, not grasping what had happened.

Smoke billowed from his breastplate.

A power and heat so strong they took his breath away told him his own magic had struck his chest. The sparks danced uselessly before him.

It rebounded—?

As flames he had never expected to experience burned his body, he stared at the being standing in the distance.

Even now, the ominous beast's armored shell was glowing.

Light rippled out from the spot on its stomach where Bell had expected the electrical fire to make contact, but there wasn't the faintest trace of a wound.

"——"

The blank incomprehension in Bell's mind lasted only an instant, but the Juggernaut seized that moment.

Crushing the ground underfoot, it launched its body forward at top speed.

"Whoaaa!!"

As the monster bore down with its right arm raised above its head, Bell switched into defensive mode just a second too late.

The long, glittering claws swept through the air.

Bell whipped the Hestia Knife from its hilt with his right hand.

The knife's purple arc mirrored that of the monster's claws as Bell tried to block the blow.

"No—"

Just as he made contact, Bell heard someone behind him whisper.

It was the despairing whisper of an elf, like a bird that had lost its wings.

Then came a blow so powerful the whole world quaked before Bell's eyes.

The next moment, he felt a lightness in his right shoulder.

"—?"

Something was spinning through the air.

It was as vibrant as a songbird, spraying specks of liquid that looked like blood.

It was sheathed in a gauntlet.

It was gripping a *black knife*.

It was Bell's right arm.

"Aa—"

He had lost one of his arms.

His right one, *sliced off at the elbow.*

It took a second for the reality to hit him.

The next instant, what remained of his arm flared like it was on fire.

"Ahhhhhhhhhhhhhhhhhhhhhhhhhhhhhhhhhhhhhhhhhhhhhhhhh!!"

A scream ripped from his throat.

As if to restart the temporarily frozen flow of time, a fountain of blood spurted from the exposed flesh of his right elbow.

The pain was so intense he thought his nerve endings were going to burn out. His eyes were bloodshot to their very core.

The arm drew a parabola through the air before landing—still clutching the knife—in the waterway.

"Mr. Cranell!"

He could hear Lyu screaming his name.

But it wasn't a cry of grief—it was a warning.

The enormous shadow covering Bell flickered.

He looked up in surprise and saw the silhouette of the monster with the claws of its left hand raised like a guillotine above his head.

The fear that flooded his body at the sight of those claws that had ripped off his arm, protector and all, was enough to make him cry. Nevertheless, he raised his gauntlet-clad left arm to block the blow. Its dual adamantite flashed.

An instant later, the gauntlet met the claws, and it was destroyed.

"—"

That armor was supposed to be unrivaled.

At the very least, Bell had believed it was. Certainly, it was the strongest armor Welf had ever forged for him. But now the dir-adamantite shield that had withstood even the blows of the black minotaur was demolished.

It couldn't fend off the blow.

Bell had intended for the claws to slide along the metal, but the moment they made contact, the force of the blow had crushed the armor.

That was how strong the Juggernaut's claws of destruction were.

They extended ominously from the end of the six fingers that signaled a monster. The fingers themselves were as thin as bones, but the tips were thick and sharp and curved. They glinted like purple jewels, just like Bell's Divine Knife.

Only Lyu and Jura knew the truth: that one must never tangle with those claws. One had to somehow fight without letting them bite into one's flesh. Only they, paralyzed by the return of their worst nightmare, knew that defense against the claws of destruction was completely impossible.

Shaped more like fangs than claws, they were a gift from the Dungeon, stronger than any armor and honed to points sharper than any weapon.

"—"

The monster advanced mercilessly on Bell as he stared in a daze at the crushed back of his left hand.

It brought its claws up into the air, then down.

That was enough to split open his armor.

Somehow managing to avoid a direct blow, his one-armed body crumpled. All hope drained from his heart as he watched the fragments of silver swirl in front of his eyes.

His shoulder guards, his hip guards, his knee guards, and his chest guard all split into fragments and flew off him. Even the leg holster on his left leg burst off, spraying blood into the air.

Whether from the extreme pain or from fear, Bell realized something through the haze of blood and tears.

The reason the monster's defenses were so low was that it had no need for them.

It had magnificent strength, all-destroying claws, and an overwhelming, unparalleled ability to kill. Why would it need to defend itself against prey it could slaughter in a single second? The entire purpose of its specialization in offensive attacks was to crush its enemies.

The monster before his eyes was catastrophe incarnate.

It was an apostle of murder let loose by the Dungeon.

Like a marionette with its strings cut, Bell was performing a clumsy dance. A black shadow was corroding his heart, even though he had managed to stay alive this long.

He could practically hear his heart being crushed.

It was the sound of a despair far deeper and more devastating than what he had felt when he faced the one-armed minotaur.

Pitilessly, the Juggernaut swept its tail—that all-destroying weapon of death—toward the prey that had stumbled in its battle stance.

It landed on Bell's neck.

"—"

A cracking sound came from a place that should never have made that sound.

—Death.

Bell heard the sound of his own life coming to an end.

He lost consciousness.

Launched into the air by the monster's tail, the boy's body flew forward like an arrow.

Blood flying from the joint where the severed arm had been, it rolled over and over across the floor and finally came to a rest where land met water.

It lay there completely still.

"...Mr....Cranell!"

Standing stock-still, Lyu was barely able to whisper those two words.

Time slowed to a crawl.

The world went flat—the scene before her very eyes, a lie. Even the water seemed to have stopped flowing. The screams of the other adventurers and the sound of her own heartbeat grew distant.

Only the horrible figure of the boy lying faceup where he had landed was fresh and bright.

"—Bell?!"

Lyu's scream was like silk being ripped. Tearing off the chains of trauma that had held her back, she half dove, half ran toward him.

"...?!"

She kneeled beside him, dumbstruck.

In addition to the severed arm, his whole armorless body was covered in deep cuts and bruises, indicating broken bones. Blood dribbled from his mouth. There was no sign of consciousness in the pair of eyes behind his bangs. Still, it was a miracle that his head was even attached to his body after suffering that fierce blow from the monster's tail.

The word *death* flitted across Lyu's mind.

Shivering and pale, she placed one finger on Bell's neck.

"...! He's still alive...?!"

Surprised, she leaned toward him. She could just barely make out the faintest sound of breathing.

The Goliath Scarf had allowed Bell to take the massive blow to his neck without suffering even a scratch. The material fashioned from the giant's wall of steel had stopped the deadly blow and saved the life of its wearer.

Although it had repelled direct damage, however, it had not been able to soften the impact. That alone had inflicted enough damage to make Bell himself think he was dying. Most likely, some of the vertebrae in his neck were fractured.

I have to stop the bleeding from that arm! No, I better do something for his neck first!

Dripping sweat, Lyu began to chant a spell.

"I sing now of a distant forest. A familiar melody of life!"

She had used up all her potions during the battle for Knossos and her pursuit of Jura's gang. The spell felt like it stretched on forever, but it was the only recovery magic she had on hand.

"Noa Heal!"

A gentle light like the dappled sun of a forest surrounded the base of Bell's neck. It was an all-purpose magic with the power to heal surface wounds, as well as other types of damage, and restore strength. However, it did not work immediately like a potion; the length of time required for full recovery was its main drawback.

As she waited for it to work, Lyu used her teeth and one arm to tear off a piece of her cape and tie it around Bell's right arm to stop the bleeding. Cursing her own failure to act at the crucial moment, she tended to the boy as if she was paying off her sin.

"Aaaaaaaaaaaaaaaaaaaaaaaaaaaaaah!!"

"!"

Having put an end to Bell, its first target, the Juggernaut had turned its attention once again to the remaining adventurers. The reason it turned toward Bors's group rather than toward Lyu or Jura was simply that there were more of them.

The storm of slaughter rose again.

"H-h-help!!"

Lyu's heart trembled at the pleas for assistance.

—I want to help them, but if I leave Mr. Cranell now—

Lyu was unable to finish her anguished thought.

In an interval too short even to call a moment of hesitation, the monster had finished its massacre. Aside from Bors and a few others who had run in the opposite direction, all the adventurers were now no more than gruesome corpses. Among them were the animal-person siblings and the Amazonian warrior Bell had tried to save.

Lyu hadn't even been granted the opportunity to make a choice.

"Yaaaaaaaaaaaaaaaaaaaaaaaaaaaaaaaaaaaaaaaaaaaaaaaaaaaaaa!!"

The moment the healing light faded, Lyu howled and dashed toward the monster, which was turned away from her. Like an insane animal, she charged forward and drove her wooden sword into its purple-blue back.

"—"

The Juggernaut responded simply.

Releasing the energy stored in its back-bent knees, it leaped momentarily out of sight. Then, clinging to the side of a crystal column, it peered at her with glowing crimson eyes as if to say, *You next?*

The next instant, it was charging her.

She dodged the razor-like claws by planting her hands on the ground.

As the hem of her long cape was shredded, she pushed away her panic and flew beast-like toward the monster, which had just landed back on the ground.

It blocked her blow with its tail, but she aimed relentlessly for its chest, drawing close to the body that caused her such powerful physical revulsion.

Tucked in where its long arms could not easily reach, she jabbed the monster again and again with her sword.

"!"

"—!"

But the extraordinarily agile monster leaped from side to side and then backward, lashing out at her in return, and very soon Lyu found herself on the defensive.

This was the reason she had so stubbornly avoided Bell at first. If the Juggernaut was once again spawned, she didn't want him to become its target.

It was a passive strategy totally unlike the normal Lyu. This was the underside of the terror that had been imprinted onto her very core. This was how deeply she was tormented by the calamity that had stolen everything from her five years ago.

"Aaaaah, aaaaaaaaaaaaaaaaaah!"

The ashen scene rose before her eyes once again.

Her companions were collapsing.

Their weapons crushed, her friends were being ripped to shreds.

They screamed as the monster ground them between its fangs.

The vicious claws had torn through the bodies of her companions.

The scenes seared into her brain, stirring up her terror and crushing her will to fight.

And so she screamed.

She screamed to cheat her fear, to obliterate the past, and to spur her body on to action.

When this scream, this outpouring of raging emotion, went dead, Lyu would no longer be able to fight. Her heart would collapse before this overwhelming being, and she would hug herself and sob like a helpless child.

Because she knew that, she flourished her wooden sword and screamed her battle cry.

"—Ha!"

The Juggernaut responded with a short breath almost like a sigh and a fierce swipe of the claws on one hand.

It was enough to send Lyu's sword flying.

"—"

Alvs Lumina, her second-tier weapon fashioned from the branch of a holy tree, burst into pieces. Following the same path as Bell's armor, it bid her good-bye.

The merciless strength that had destroyed her weapon generated an impact that fractured the fingers gripping the sword's handle. Lyu went flying through the air and landed with a crash on the crystal floor, faceup.

The breath was forced from her lungs in a single gust.

"*Gaaarrr!* Now! Now's your chance! Get that bastard!!"

Far away from her, Bors let out a battle cry.

The remaining adventurers knew escape was hopeless. In the time that Lyu had bought them, they began to chant—in other words, to release a Concurrent Bombardment. Bors, too, took part, wielding his magic blade even as terror pulled him downward.

"No, stop!!"

Lyu's words did not reach them. She could barely even breathe.

As her futile cry faded, the purple-blue shell encasing the Juggernaut's huge frame glowed.

Just like a replay of what happened when Bell tried to use a Firebolt on the monster, the magic attack bounced back toward its source. Only this time, it was not a single Firebolt but a far more powerful Concurrent Bombardment.

"—"

It hit them head-on.

The Juggernaut's protective shell had the power of magic reflection. It was the sole shield of this monster that had traded defense for the power of annihilation. Even if an adventurer was to release automatic homing magic, which was ordinarily a fail-proof method of hitting a target, it would not make contact with the Juggernaut.

The adventurers were thus cut off from the magic they had counted on as their ultimate safety net. Anyone would lose heart under these despairing circumstances, just as *Astrea Familia* had done five years earlier.

Fortunately, Bors was at the back of the party and avoided a direct hit. He stared in a daze at his charred companions. His eye patch had been torn off and his empty left eye socket was exposed, but he had no time to worry about that. The monster was bearing down on him, its own eye sockets glowing.

"*Stoppppppppppppppppppppppppppppppppppppp!!*" Bors sobbed.

Thrusting both hands in front of him, unable even to stand up, he pissed his pants.

Even for a second-tier adventurer like Bors, this monster was too much to face.

The claws descended toward him.

"—aaa."

Drawing a vivid arc, they moved from the top of his head straight down.

He didn't even have time to think back on his life. But his brain registered the sound of his own body splitting into two halves. He heard his head being crushed, his flesh being torn, and his bones being pulverized.

It was over in an instant. Bors was dead.

"Stand up!"

"—!!"

The fog of hallucination cleared.

As Bors recovered from the vision his petrified brain had produced, he found himself alive, with an elf fighting in his place. Before the all-destroying claws had reached him, the elf had intercepted the blow with one of her own, delivered to the monster's forearm. She was now fighting it desperately with two daggers.

At that very moment, the elf was protecting Bors.

"Escape, quick!"

"Y-you…"

Bors's word trailed off as he stared at the profile of the female adventurer, from which the hood and mask had fallen away.

It was the very same brave elf he had seen before on the eighteenth floor. The precise elf who had fought single-handedly against the terrifying black giant.

Just then, the monster brought up its claws with ferocious speed.

Lyu bent backward, just barely avoiding a direct hit, but the claws nevertheless grazed her, ripping open her shoulder.

A geyser of blood spouted from the elf's thin body.

As the warm liquid spattered Bors's face, Lyu clenched her teeth and resisted her body's urge to crumple to the ground.

"Hurryyyyyyyyyyyyyyyyyy!!"

"Aaaaaaaaaaaaaaaaaaaaaaaaaaaaaaaaaaaaaaaaaaaaaah!!"

Bors fled, his feet flapping noisily against the ground.

Stumbling repeatedly over himself, he was making no progress whatsoever. To protect him, Lyu—her face covered in a gory makeup of blood—took the brunt of the Juggernaut's attack herself.

"!!"

"Oof!"

Its long tail beat against her legs.

Although it lacked the menace of the claws, the hard appendage covered in its black and purplish-blue shell was no different from a cudgel.

Lyu's right leg, encased in its long boot, snapped like a twig under the blow. Her shinbone let out a dry popping sound as she flew into the air.

"Ah—!"

Lyu gripped her awkwardly bent leg with one hand as she cried out in wordless agony.

She felt she would faint from the unbelievable pain. But she knew she could not.

Stomp! The horrifying sound of the monster's immense body advancing toward her rang through the room.

"No…!"

As a crystal fragment bore into her left cheek, she lifted her trembling face.

Aside from her writhing form, there was no other sign of life in the sprawling room. Even Jura was gone. Had he escaped? She could no longer fully understand what was going on.

Destruction advanced.

Despair bore down on her in the form of the Juggernaut.

She was covered in wounds from head to toe. As it landed before her eyes, she realized she had no way left to defend herself against it.

I couldn't stop Jura's schemes, and now here I am, my shameful failure exposed...

She felt humiliated. She wanted to scream and cry. She wanted to place a deadly curse on herself for once again making a mistake that led to calamity.

She still hadn't explained anything to Syr and her coworkers. She hadn't done anything to repay them for giving her a home. She had to survive, if only to explain herself to them.

...Oh, but...

If I die here, I can be with Alize and the others...

At last, she could be beside her companions once again.

At last, she could apologize to them.

At last, she could let them castigate her.

Finally, this sin of killing them will be...

At last, she would be free of the guilt she had hidden in the furthest depths of her heart.

For Lyu, that would be a kind of salvation.

It would be a sort of ceremony in which she buried the self whose dishonor had been exposed.

A smile of resignation curled her lips.

A tear fell from one sky-blue eye.

The scale of her heart tipped from attachment to life toward the peace of death.

"Huh?"

Just then, something caught Lyu's eye.

Shrieks were ringing out—the death songs of adventurers.

Screams were echoing—the will of the elf who fought and suffered yet refused to succumb to fear.

Bell's finger twitched at the sounds of the battlefield.

A tremor slightly stronger than the others carved a crack in the crystal ground, shattered it, and sent Bell's body sliding from the border between water and land into the water.

Below the surface, sounds were muffled. A crimson fog spread from his severed arm. He sank toward the cold depths of the waterway.

"—Bell."

A tearful voice reached him as he drifted slowly downward.

Her emerald-blue hair swirling, the mermaid reached out her hand toward the pitifully wounded boy. She was hugging his right arm, still gripping the knife, to her chest. She sank her teeth into her own wrist. As she pressed the arm against the surface from which it had been severed, it absorbed her lifeblood.

Healing bubbles floated around Bell's body as it regained its missing limb.

"Bell…Bell."

The mermaid's tears were unending.

Placing a hand on the cheek of the boy whose eyes remained closed, she took his knife and slashed herself over and over again. She held the sinking body tight against her own.

Her blood ran into Bell's wounds, melting into him. Surrounded by a haze of crimson produced by their intermingled blood, his battered body began to recover.

"Live," the monster girl whispered over and over again.

"Open your eyes," she murmured into his ear.

He responded.

"Oh!!"

He clenched his hands into fists, opened his eyes, and spewed out countless bubbles.

The black knife glittered with renewed life.

He stared into the tear-drenched eyes of the mermaid, so close to him their foreheads were touching.

Thank you.

I'm sorry.

I have to go.

The boy who mouthed these words, the boy whom Mari loved, was not a prince on a shipwrecked boat.

He was an adventurer.

For the sake of his companion who was still fighting, he had to revive his despair-riddled heart. He had to light the flames of recovery.

Tears trickling down her cheeks, Mari reached out a hand to stop him and then drew it back.

The boy was stubborn. He was an adventurer. Mari would do the same thing to save the family she loved. So instead of holding him back, she hugged him one more time. Then, quietly, she let him go.

Released from the mermaid's arms, Bell kicked and surged upward.

"Promise me—"

Mari cried as she watched the figure move farther and farther from her. Reaching her hand toward him, she sent her wish into the world of water.

"—Promise me you won't lose."

Bell extended a fist and broke through the water's surface where the light filtered in.

Lyu saw everything.

She saw the drops of water flying, the form bursting powerfully through the water's surface, and the foot stepping firmly onto the crystal ground.

She saw the boy standing on land.

She saw the light of determination in his rubellite eyes.

"Thank you, Mari."

Mermaid lifeblood. The mysterious drop item was said to have the power to heal wounds. And truly, Bell had fully recovered. Smoke

rose from the wounds that had been bathed in the blood of her self-sacrifice.

To Lyu's eyes, the scene looked like a beacon for a counterattack.

His right arm restored, Bell steeled his will and tightened his grip on the black knife.

"—"

Behind the Juggernaut, who stood stock-still, before Lyu, who looked on in astonishment, and beside Mari, who poked her face from the water, Bell flew into a rage.

"!!"

He raced toward the Juggernaut, his body—just moments before on the verge of death—transformed now into a speeding bullet.

"!!"

The monster spun violently around as Lyu watched. It had determined that this revenger, whom it had destroyed beyond all recovery but who now came dancing back to life, was no mere bit of prey but rather its prime enemy, worthy of complete annihilation.

As the boy charged toward it with terrifying speed, the monster flourished its claws powerfully, as if to say, *This time, you must be crushed.*

"—!!"

Faced with this deadly blow that approached at lightning speed, Bell chose not escape but direct advance.

He tore the scarf from his neck, wrapped it around his left hand, and shot forward.

"?!"

Astonishment flickered in the Juggernaut's glowing orbs.

The black scarf that Bell had wrapped around his hand in place of the demolished gauntlet threw off a shower of sparks as the monster's claws *slid over it.*

The devastating weapon bestowed upon the monster by the Dungeon was deflected by the ultimate defensive armor born of that very same Dungeon.

As if to pay back the monster in its own currency, Bell snatched its brief moment of hesitation to attack.

With a suddenness and speed that left no room for escape, the Hestia Knife glinted backhand toward the monster's chest.

"?!"

Next it was Bell's turn to be astonished.

He had ripped into his enemy's chest. Yet the response did not suggest he had crushed its core.

In other words, *it had no magic stone*?!

Shuddering at each other's menacing presences, boy and monster slid cleanly past each other.

Instantly, both turned on their heels. Their gazes clashed. Their respective blows met thin air.

This was when the life-or-death battle truly began.

"—!!"

"Yah!"

As the Juggernaut howled murderously, Bell gave a spirited shout and charged head-on toward the monster, Goliath Scarf and Hestia Knife at the ready.

The monster sprang away rapidly with a series of jumps fueled by the energy stored in its reverse-joint knees.

I'll be slaughtered before I can blink if I let it use those legs to its advantage.

Bell chose instead to engage in a bullfight.

Pouring every drop of his strength into the opening blow in hopes of getting a head start on his opponent, he turned his body into a pure-white arrow of light.

"—?!"

The monster charged forward even as its enemy's lancing attack shaved the surface of its neck and shoulder.

Blood, flesh, and skin flew.

As Lyu looked on, dumbfounded, and Mari clapped both hands over her mouth, Bell launched a special attack propelled by his surging blood.

"Aaaaaaaaaaaa!!"

The black knife was aimed at the monster's right knee joint.

With inhuman speed, the blade cut into its target.

"?!"

The Juggernaut's right leg dropped slightly with a loud *thump.*

Although its battle stance and ability to continue fighting had not been impacted in the least, it was no longer able to fly about at lightning speed like a hurricane. Bell's single blow had landed perfectly on the source of those powerful jumps: the monster's reverse-joint knees.

It stared intently at Bell, who had already suffered serious damage in their clashes. Though the left half of his body was soaked in blood, the adventurer's eyes sent a clear message: *We're just getting started.*

"Game on!"

Bell raised his knife, his rubellite eyes flashing.

"—OOO!!"

The monster's crimson eyes burned. For the first time, it howled with rage.

It charged forward, the exploding swirl of crystal fragments from the floor obscuring its opponent's form.

Just as Bell had anticipated, the close-range fight began.

"Mr. Cranell?!" Lyu screamed as she propped herself into a sitting position, her broken leg beneath her, and watched his reckless venture unfold.

Lyu knew the terror of the Juggernaut better than anyone else.

What Bell was doing may have been his only choice, but nevertheless it was crazy to place oneself within the monster's sphere of slaughter. Moment by moment, she could see his body being battered and wounded.

Blood and chunks of flesh flew as his undershirt—stripped of its protective armor—was ripped to shreds. With every passing second, he was being shaved away. Mari watched in pale silence.

But—

"...?!"

The claws of destruction did not pierce Bell's body.

Using the scarf wrapped around his left hand exactly like a

gauntlet, he deflected the Juggernaut's claws by sliding them over its tough surface.

Again and again, the monster brought down its deadliest weapon, as if to say, *Stop playing with me.*

But the scarf would not shatter. The number of scratches on its surface increased, but the armor of the Goliath—the "shield" that Cassandra had requested and Welf had made for him—did not break.

And as long as it did not break, Bell could keep fighting.

As long as he had the shield his friends had made for him, he could face this strongest and most terrible of calamities.

If he could withstand the deadly blows that no adventurer was supposed to be able to withstand, then he could extract the tiniest of chances at victory, and therefore he could defeat his own despair.

Screech!!

The Hestia Knife let out its own battle cry as it deflected the course of the claws. A fountain of sparks danced into the air as the blade screamed. Still, the Divine Knife did not crumble. It continued to clash with the monster's weapon.

The Juggernaut was mad with destructive rage. Bell, too, was acting out a desperate battle armed with the strongest of all blades and shields.

It's just like I suspected.

As his wounds spurted fresh blood, Bell squinted at his opponent.

He's faster than I am.

He was not only stronger but also *quicker*. Compared to the Juggernaut, everything about Bell was inferior. In the past, no matter how much higher his opponent's level had been, Bell had always had the upper hand in terms of speed and agility. Now even that advantage was gone.

Yet he did not give up in the face of this hopeless analysis. Instead, his heart cried out unyieldingly.

How could he resist this monster that surpassed him in every way? Of course, it was obvious.

By using the skill and tactics he had cultivated so far.

This was the true weapon and shield given to him as an adventurer—this determination burning in his chest. Adventurers took the trial called "despair" and transformed it into great achievement.

Its power and potential are unbelievable for its size—

If he had been asked to compare the Black Goliath and the Juggernaut, Bell honestly wouldn't have been able to say which was superior.

Comparing them was meaningless.

They worked in entirely different ways.

The Goliath had an extraordinary ability to suppress armies, while the Juggernaut was a slaughterer who excelled in inflicting deadly damage on individual adventurers. In terms of getting the job done with a single weapon, the claws of destruction most likely outdid the Goliath's hammer and howl.

On the other hand, in terms of ability to endure attacks, the Juggernaut couldn't hold a candle to the floor boss.

This monster was best able to exercise its full potential—its highly developed strength, speed, and ability to kill—not in a wide-open room but in the passageways and other closed-in spaces of the Dungeon. This made it the ideal apostle of murder, designed solely to wipe out "viruses" that damaged the Dungeon.

Is it even faster than my greatest rival?

There was the fierce, swift speed of its attacks and the constant vibrating shock waves that made his feet and hands go numb.

In a corner of Bell's burning mind, fragments of logic compared the beast he faced now to the black minotaur.

In terms of destructive power, the Juggernaut was superior because of its claws.

But perhaps Asterios was the victor when it came to physical strength?

That time, the massive bull had been on the verge of death. His true strength was probably much greater—

Bell cut off the irrelevant thoughts that flashed briefly through his mind. In this desperate battle, any unnecessary mental noise could lead directly to death. The tiniest mistake on the part of either combatant could cost them their head.

"—!"

Even as Bell's storm of knife blows wounded its body, the Juggernaut showed no sign of easing its own attack.

His whole body was screaming. His overheated limbs and trunk felt like they were about to burst apart.

His left arm might as well be shouting its death cries. Inside the Goliath Scarf, his hand had been pulverized by the force of the repeated claw attacks it had deflected. Pain was the only sense he had left. The blood was sloshing around noisily inside the wrapping. Still, Bell knew that the moment he stopped deflecting the claws, he was done for.

His shoulder and neck burned where the flesh had been gouged out.

His once-healed wounds were torn open again, gushing blood.

Still, the light glowed in his eyes, and he moved forward.

If he fell now, he was sure the Juggernaut would kill Lilly and the rest of his party. Every adventurer in the Water Capital would be exterminated.

He couldn't let it happen. He had to defend them to the death.

In other words—

You're going down!!

Even if this monster had been called forth by an Evil and Bell had never wanted to fight it, he could not leave something so destructive to its own devices.

Was he going to let it kill more people? Was he going to let the death continue?

Bell donned the mask of the hypocrite.

For the sake of the people he wanted to protect, he would kill the being in front of him.

"!!"

His enemy's attack began. Crystal fragments flew. Bell was forced into a defensive stance.

Claw swipe, dodge, biting fangs, intercept.

A counterblow from Bell, blocked by the enemy. Too shallow. Not yet. Another blow. Pieces of the enemy's shell fell away. *I'll bury it in blows.*

Bell Cranell still has fight left in him yet. Yes! Go on! For her sake! Why did I come to this floor in the first place?

In a moment that stretched on for an eternity, Bell speeded up at the literal cost of shaving away his own life.

Faster, faster, faster!

He was determined to put an end to her nightmare.

"*AAAAAAA!!*" Bell howled, blood streaming from his entire body.

He slashed toward the hurricane of death, a single piece of cloth—his only safety net—wrapped around one hand.

He faced head-on the beast that for Lyu symbolized pure despair.

He understood only a fragment of the suffering she had endured. But it was enough to set his own once-despairing heart on fire.

He howled a long howl, because that sound was the flame of his spirit that would burn away tragedy and calamity.

"Mr. Cranell..."

Even the rather insensitive Lyu knew who he was yelling for. The hotness in the depths of her chest expanded.

"...You're so much..."

Her final whispered word—"stronger"—disappeared into the din of the battlefield.

She felt pitiful lying there doing nothing. But still this feeling burned in her heart.

For the first time, she understood why Bell liked those hero's tales so much. For the first time, the elf saw how noble heroes looked when they challenged despair itself.

"...?"

The Juggernaut was puzzled by this totally new feeling it was experiencing. The white flame that had been extinguished roared back to life, had been slashed but was now charging forward, had been beaten down but rose once more in defiance. The newborn monster was unable to grasp the fact that its enemy's spirit was dominating its own.

Finally—either because it recognized the unending series of slashing attacks as a menace or because it was overwhelmed by the boy's determination—the monster for the first time retreated.

It had folded first in the life-or-death contest of endurance.

Perhaps it was due to instinct, or perhaps it was the inevitable outcome. In any case, it saw no need to risk its own life for a bit of prey that had nearly died once and was already half-dead again. And so, the monster stepped back from the close-range fight into which it had been tricked.

It was, without a doubt, an advantageous move. But Bell saw a chance for victory.

It's retreating.

Delirious and covered in blood, he nevertheless felt his hunger for battle burn with fresh ferocity. He let his mind follow the path of that desire.

His greatest rival had not retreated.

His idol would always fight to the end.

The monster before him was neither warrior nor adventurer. Bell smiled.

He had lured the Juggernaut into close combat in order to wrench this one moment from it. Although it was faster than Bell, it had been forced into the defensive for the first time in order to retreat.

He thrust his scarf-wrapped left hand toward his backward-leaning enemy.

"Firebolt!!"

Seventeen successive shots.

He concentrated his mind into those seventeen shots, loading every last drop of magical power he had into the rapid-fire attack.

The all-out, instantaneous firepower erupted before the eyes of the surprised monster.

"!"

Of course, the Juggernaut pulsed its shell to exercise its power of magic reflection. Bell's magic was pitilessly repulsed by the invincible shield.

"Yeah!!"

It fell for it!

Letting out a yell of victory, Bell *dove toward* the whirlwind of electrifying flames that came hurtling back toward him.

"?!"

Lyu couldn't believe her eyes. Mari yelped, and even the monster stared in shock.

The barrage of seventeen Firebolts sped toward him. An instant later, his body was engulfed in deep-red light.

Even as his own fire seared his flesh and pierced his flank, Bell sped forward, shouting victoriously.

A single shot.

A single, carefully aimed Firebolt exploded into his black knife.

He was *charging his weapon*.

The Juggernaut saw it—saw that instead of scattering like it should have when it hit the knife, the Firebolt was pressed into place by a white light and *focused*.

A Dual Charge.

Bell had anticipated that his Firebolt would be repulsed and used that to prepare for his deadly strike.

The massive barrage of fire provided a cover. In the moment that the raging electrical fire obscured his body from the enemy's view, he drew close to its massive frame.

The Juggernaut, frozen for just an instant, understood everything.

It had been lured into using its magic reflection by a barrage of firepower strong enough to inflict deadly injury even on a monster. It had been attacked with the aim of provoking that tiny moment of immobility caused by the use of its armored shell.

Time froze for the Juggernaut as it stared at the raging Divine Knife encased in an armor of flames.

It knew it was in a bad situation. Things were moving fast. Still, it had time. If it gathered all its strength, it could intercept the attack, defend itself, and escape.

But a kind of static was interfering with the monster's instincts.

Was that magic, or was it a knife attack? Should it deflect it with the invincible armor or destroy it with the deadly claws?

The apostle of murder was confused.

It chose escape.

Using its one remaining reverse-joint leg, it sprang forward—not perfectly but adequately.

"—"

To get straight to the point, the monster of calamity lost its bargain with the adventurer.

The second or two it spent deciding what to do was, for the Juggernaut, *a most regrettable opening* that it should never have yielded to the lightning-fast rabbit.

"*—Yaah!*"

Bell suddenly unfurled the scarf wrapped around his left hand, launching it forward.

Unlike the Firebolt, this was a midrange, indirect attack.

The black strip of fabric undulated through the air like a whip, landing on the monster's long tail.

"?!"

There was a tremendous shock as the scarf unfurled to its full length and Bell planted both feet on the crystal ground.

The Juggernaut froze unnaturally in midair. Then inertia brought it hurtling toward Bell's left hand, which still gripped the scarf.

There was the sound of muscle ripping and the snap of an arm bone popping out of place.

Bell's eyes bulged.

Still, he gathered his remaining strength and drew his left arm in toward his body.

"*Yaaaaaaaaaaaaaaaaaaaaaaaaaaaaaaaaaaaaaaaaaaaaaaaaaaaaaaaaaaaaaaaaaaaaaaaaaaaaaaaaaaaaaaaaaa!!*"

The Juggernaut—its tail entangled in the scarf—was pulled toward him. As the enormous form landed at Bell's feet, it shuddered. The monster realized the nature of the emotion it had been feeling for the past few minutes.

This was the terror that its prey experienced.

"—?!"

As if to shake off the feeling, it pulsed its shell with purplish-blue light. In the face of the flaming knife in its enemy's right hand, it brandished its own weapon—its all-destroying claws, the claws that nothing could withstand.

A moment earlier, it had wondered whether the knife would deliver magic or an ordinary slashing attack. The answer was neither. The deadly blow it held in wait would allow for neither reflection nor defense.

It was a sacred flame that would turn all to ash.

Bell had charged it for nine seconds.

As the Juggernaut towered over him with claws bared, Bell unleashed the blow.

"Argo Vesta!!"

A blast of light.

"—"

Thundering flames swallowed the enormous fang-like claws.

A flare extinguished the flashing purplish-blue light.

The claws of destruction shattered. Black and purple fragments flew everywhere.

Bell had been thrown backward, but he kept his right arm extended. This time, it was the Juggernaut's right arm that would be obliterated.

"AAAAAAAAAAAAAAAAAAAAAAAAAAAAAAAAAAAAAAAAAAAAAAAAAAAAAAAAAAAAAAAAAAAAA!!"

The monster wailed.

Its right arm had vanished, claws and all, in the roar and flash of the sacred flame. The shock reverberated through its shoulder and into the right half of the towering body.

Its speed and aggression were extraordinarily developed, but its endurance and defense were correspondingly low. Fissures ran down its flank and back, and chunks of shell clattered onto the floor. As its fossil-like form crumbled, the Juggernaut crashed into the crystal floor.

Its right arm blasted off and its tail finally freed from the bonds of the scarf, it rolled and scraped across the floor, finally coming to a halt in the center of the room.

For the first time in its life, the Juggernaut howled in grief.

I didn't charge enough…!

Bell squinted at the writhing, shrieking monster. Although it was inevitable due to the short amount of time he'd had, the blow hadn't been deadly.

But he could do something about that. He could bury a silver round in the hideous beast.

"Owwwwwwwwww…!!"

A terrifying jolt of pain shot through Bell's left hand.

His mind had robbed his body of strength in its tremendous effort to achieve both Swift-Strike Magic and a Dual Charge. His legs were shaking. His arms felt like they were about to be torn from his shoulders. He now couldn't feel his left hand.

But he had to fight. He had to pull together his last drops of strength. He had to put a stop to that monster and its whirlwind of calamity.

As the maelstrom of pain forced a tear from his eye, Bell gripped the Hestia Knife and turned toward the Juggernaut, still prone on the floor.

"—Mr. Cranell?!"

Lyu, who had been watching in a daze as this scene unfolded, shuddered and let out a cry.

Bell noticed, too, but it was too late.

A one-armed shadow leaped from behind a crystal column and fell over the Juggernaut.

"Ha-ha-ha-ha-ha-ha-ha-ha!! I did it!"

It was Jura.

The tamer had been hiding and waiting for this moment to reappear.

The magic collar, still encircling the monster's thin, bony neck, pulsed with a strange crimson light.

"I didn't expect you to bring it to its knees like that!"

"Jura…!"

"But with this, it's mine!"

Trembling with joy, the catman grinned at the dumbfounded Bell and Lyu.

This was the long-cherished moment he had been waiting for. Sneering, he pulled out his crimson whip and lashed it powerfully against the ground.

"Stand, monster of mine! Kill Leon and that brat!!"

The collar pulsed with a bright light in response to the whip. As the magic item flashed wildly, the Juggernaut's half-destroyed body convulsed again and again…until finally, slowly, it rose.

The crimson light in the depths of its eye sockets bore into Bell and Lyu.

Bell grimaced, unable to hide his fear in the face of a monster whose eyes—as if insensate to all the injuries it had suffered—were filled with pure bloodlust.

"Ha-ha-ha-ha-ha! Yes, kill them! Kill them both! With those claws of yours—"

The next instant, the monster swung the remains of its tail, as if in irritation.

Chunks of flesh flew. The catman's body was cleaved in two.

In the end, Jura never knew what had happened. The upper half of his body flew through the air and landed with a splash in the waterway flowing through the room. As if realizing its fate, the lower half toppled over. Red bubbles frothed as the upper half sank into the water.

Bell and Lyu gaped in silence.

The end of the Evil had come so abruptly.

"—, —, —…!!"

But the collar kept pulsing with light.

As if illuminated by the dead man's last wish—or, rather, his rancor—the collar continued to flash, animating the Juggernaut's body. The battered legs took a step toward Bell.

"Uh…!"

In the face of this destroyer who seemed to take no notice of its own injuries, Bell flourished the Hestia Knife. He let out a battle cry, as if to whip his exhausted body toward one last battle.

"Huh?"

Just then, he heard a crumbling sound. Or more accurately, the sound of piled-up rubble being swept aside.

Something pulled at Bell's mind. Even though the Juggernaut was right in front of him now, he obeyed his adventurer's instinct and turned his head toward the sound that indicated something abnormal in the Dungeon.

Directly behind him was Lyu, still unable to stand.

Behind her, slithering from the pile of crystal rubble, was a giant serpent monster.

"—"

The lambton was supposed to be dead.

But there it was, as huge as ever, the pulsing collar around its neck clearly responding to the tamer's command. Its multiple bloodied eyes glared as it obeyed the last command of its master.

Kill Leon and that brat!

The near-dead serpent roared and bore down behind Lyu, scattering crystal fragments as it approached.

"Miss Lyu!!"

Her eyes widened as she realized what was happening, but it was too late. The lambton was charging forward, its enormous maw wide open.

Bell ran toward it.

With the little energy he had left, he accelerated, grabbed Lyu's outstretched hand, and pulled her close.

A moment later, both adventurers were engulfed in the serpent's mouth.

"OOOOOOOOOOOOOOOOOOOOOOOOOOOOOOOOOOOOOOOOOOOO!!"

As it bellowed, the lambton burrowed its sharply pointed head into the ground. Its corkscrewing body crushed through the bedrock as it drilled and gouged downward.

"—!!"

The Juggernaut followed. Roaring and scattering pieces of shell from its fractured body, it dove into the hole that the lambton had made.

The heroic battle that had unfolded in the crystal room was over.

"Bell…Beeeell?!"

Just one living being remained.

The mermaid's sorrowful cry echoed through the now-quiet space.

"Please let me go, Miss Cassandra! Enough already…!"

Lilly's shout disappeared into the din of the Great Falls.

They were in the cavern on the twenty-fifth floor. Standing on the cliff near the mouth of the falls that overlooked the cavern on the floor below, the adventurers argued among themselves.

"No, you can't go…! Not to the twenty-seventh floor…!"

Cassandra was holding on fiercely to the prum's arm. She pushed away Mikoto, who was tearfully trying to hold her back, and gripped Lilly's small hand. Her face was so transformed as she struggled to keep *Hestia Familia* from moving on that they didn't know what to make of it.

My dream has come true after all! I can't let them go! Their deaths have been foretold…!

All her actions were driven by that one thought. Guilt and despair overwhelmed her. The countless souls she had abandoned to death were tormenting her conscience and weighing on her heart. Her chest felt tight and warm, like her own thoughts were chewing away at her. Tears spilled from her eyes.

But, but, if they don't go…

She could save them. As long as they stayed there, the people Cassandra cared about would be safe. This would not absolve her of her sins, but the thought nevertheless brought Cassandra some relief.

If she kept them there, she could avoid total destruction.

But then, as if the Dungeon were sneering at Cassandra, a tremor shook the ground.

"—"

An earthquake? No, a shaking caused by the Dungeon.

Welf and the others, who had been so troubled by Cassandra's strange behavior, froze.

The sound was unmistakable.

"Hey, that noise…!"

"You're kidding me…!

"It's impossible. I mean, one was just spawned two weeks ago!"

The Dungeon ignored the sudden paleness of Ouka's, Welf's, and Lilly's faces and continued its groans.

It had only one thought.

It had sent out its apostle of murder, its equivalent of an immune system, yet the virus remained alive. Even worse, the child of calamity had left the floor, despite the fact that the contaminants destroying its mother's womb remained in the Water Capital.

Not just one or two but a number so large it couldn't be ignored.

The Dungeon could not overlook this.

So it made a completely improbable decision. Raising its voice in a howl, it spawned *that* thing.

"Th-th-this is…"

Lilly and the others recognized something—something in the signs that an unbelievably huge being was about to be spawned, in the tremors that shook the floor and the sound of enormous fissures splitting the walls.

"It's coming!" Aisha screamed.

The next instant, the Great Falls on the twenty-seventh floor exploded. Huge jets of water spouted up to the twenty-fifth floor, beating down onto the cavern like a pounding rain.

This subterranean rain poured onto the thing that burst through the falls on the lowest floor, wrapping its form in smoky white mist. Slowly, it sank toward the bottom of the plunge pool.

A moment later, it burst up again.

Then it began to literally climb the several-hundred-meder-tall column of raging water that was the Great Falls.

"—"

As Cassandra looked down on the chilling form that rose from the twenty-seventh to the twenty-sixth floor, and then toward the twenty-fifth, she remembered something.

Oh, don't worry, monsters don't climb up the falls.

Well, most *don't.*

A certain Amazon had said those words just a few days before. The very same Amazon who stood beside her now, *podao* at the ready and eyes filled with astonishment. Cassandra finally understood what she had meant.

"Get baaaaaaaaaaaaaaaaaaaaaaaaaaaaaaaaaaaaaaaaaaaaaaaaaaaaaaack!!" Welf screamed. The entire group sprang away from the cliff's edge that formed the mouth of the falls.

No sooner had they done so than it shattered apart. The tsunami that surged from it swallowed them all and carried them toward the back of the bank.

One by one, they stood up; raised their drenched, coughing faces; and looked at the two-headed dragon before them.

"The Monster Rex of the twenty-seventh floor—" Lilly whispered in a daze.

Aisha spit out the rest of the sentence.

"—Amphisbaena."

As if answering its mother's call, the huge floor boss writhing in the center of the twenty-fifth-floor plunge pool looked up.

"Oooooooooooooooooooooooooooooooooooooooooooooooo!"

The Amphisbaena was an anomaly among floor bosses known to the Guild. Contravening the rule that confined Monster Rexes to the guarding of a specific floor, this one was mobile.

As her companions scowled and brandished their weapons, Cassandra stared absentmindedly.

This was the Dungeon, the crucible of monsters.

The limitless Dungeon, for which the rebellion of a prophetess of tragedy was a mere trifling matter.

The two-headed white monster roared with the will of that Dungeon.

Cassandra's face froze.

She and her party may have escaped catastrophe, but they were now facing—yes, despair.

CHAPTER 6
AND SO THEY SPIN THEIR CRUEL FATE

The sound of bedrock being shattered rang out.
The huge form descended in a rain of rock and stone.
The terrific sound of that form ripping through the air was succeeded by that of it crashing into the earth.
The whole floor shook.
Beyond the veil of smoke, a long bluish-white body writhed in the newly formed depression.
It was a wormwell, that enormous serpent monster.
"—Aa!!"
The lambton raged.
Its multiple eyes crushed and bleeding, it flailed as if it was suffering the cruelest torment imaginable. A red-streaked liquid spilled from its enormous jaws as its long body floundered on the ground.
It looked precisely like a child who had eaten some foreign object guaranteed to cause it a royal stomachache.
Suddenly, its body convulsed with a loud *thump*. It happened again and then again, four times in total.
Each time, its cries grew more desperate. The bluish-white surface of its body glowed pale pink, as if it were being illuminated from inside by a lamp. Finally, tremors overtook its whole body, and the light of an electrifying flame pulsed forth.
Once, twice it pulsed, and still it did not stop.
A blazing column of electrical fire rose from the flank of the lambton's body.
With a roaring crash, the monster—burned open from the inside—rolled over sideways, sapped of all strength.
And then, from the center of the beast's long form, a black knife burst through the skin. It was as if a sword were growing from the inside of the wormwell's body. The hieroglyphs engraved into the blade glowed

with light. With a horrifying sound of ripping flesh, it sawed ever downward.

A vertical slash appeared in the skin.

The monster's guts tumbled out with a gush of crimson water. They were followed by a pair of hands, which grabbed the edges of the wound and pulled with all their might to the right and left.

"Uwaaaaaaaaaaaaaaaaaaaaaaaaaaaaaaaaaaaaaaaaaaaaaaaaa...!"

A white-haired boy appeared.

Squinting, steam rising from his body, Bell screamed. He stumbled forward a few steps from the prison of the lambton's body, then fell flat on his face into the puddle of reddish liquid.

"Ahhhhhhhhhhh!!"

His entire body was *melting*. His exposed skin and parts of his adventurer's gear seemed to have dissolved, and his white hair was smoking. The only part of him that was unharmed was the black scarf wrapped around his left hand and the weapon that had been protected by its sheath.

He had been burned by the potent poisonous acid inside the stomach of the monster that had swallowed him. As the cool air bathed his skin now that he had finally escaped, a searing pain engulfed his whole body. And since he was lying facedown in a pool of blood mixed with stomach acid, his skin was being burned all over again.

Despite the pain, he planted his hands on the ground and pushed his body up, then stood unsteadily.

"Miss Lyu...Miss Lyuuuuuuuuuuuuuuuuuuuuuuuuuuuuuuuu?!"

Prying open an eyelid that had been glued shut and looking around at the blurred scene in front of him, he turned toward the monster. Then, with an earsplitting moan, he plunged back into its stomach.

A moment later, he emerged again, an elf wrapped in his arms.

"Blehhhhhh!"

Had they been ordinary people, they would long ago have melted together into a single amiable puddle in the monster's gut.

But they were not ordinary people. They were upper-class adventurers who had been elevated three times to a higher level. They had been able to withstand the bath of powerful stomach acid.

Bell dragged Lyu—who was half-sitting, half-standing, and entirely helpless—around the puddle of blood and then collapsed onto the ground.

Lyu was completely drained of strength. Although Bell had protected her after they were swallowed by holding her close to his body, her long cape and battle clothes were partially dissolved. Her pliant elf's skin, too, was horribly marred by burns. Her eyes were shut tight as if in eternal sleep.

A tear fell from Bell's eye. By now he was moving through pure effort of will. He knelt beside her and lifted her body in his arms.

"Miss Lyu, Miss Lyu?! Please, please open your eyes...!"

With shaking hands and fingers that sloughed off skin, he gripped her shoulders. Again and again, he called out her name, as if to tie her to the world of the living.

Whether in response to his pleading it was not clear, but the lashes of her tightly closed eyes trembled.

"Miss Lyu...!"

But as soon as joy flooded his face—

A monster howled, crushing his hopes.

"—"

Yanked back to reality, Bell slowly raised his head.

They were in a vast room. It was inconceivably enormous. Just too huge.

Peering nervously around his dim surroundings, Bell tried to comfort himself with the thought that he did not see any monsters nearby, but he could not feel at ease.

If we're attacked by a monster now, this will all end.

No, that's wrong.

Where are we?

What floor are we on?

He knew that wormwells could move between floors. He had been repeatedly jolted back and forth in the pitch-black of its stomach and tossed about by the impact of its digging. However, he had no way of knowing just how far the monster that now lay dead beside him had burrowed.

Most likely, he was somewhere below the twenty-seventh floor.

As he dug his fingers into Lyu's shoulders and held her tightly to protect her from harm, he tried to beat back the terror long enough to figure out what was going on.

The ground was made of dirt and stone. Far in the distance, he could see that the same was true of the walls. The open space above his head was exceedingly high, so much so that he could not see the ceiling even with his Level Four eyesight.

He was trapped in a vast darkness.

The only source of light was the luminescence glowing at even intervals along the walls. The ground, the walls, and the floor itself were all *cloudy white*.

An icy draft blew past Bell, assaulting his neck as if to whisper, *Finally figured it out, have you?*

The gloomy darkness that sat heavily on his shoulders began to laugh into his ears.

His heart was pounding deafeningly. He felt like it was going to burst through his ribs and come flying out of his body.

It took him several seconds to realize that the continuous rasping sound, like someone blowing a hoarse whistle, was actually his own uneven breath.

No way. No way. No. Way.

His instincts were screaming at him, but his rational mind wanted to deny the truth.

The knowledge he had stocked away in his memory during his time studying with Eina told him that his current surroundings were a cruelly perfect fit for the description of a certain floor.

The structure of the space was overwhelmingly gargantuan. The scale was so different it made him want to cry.

This was not the scale of the upper levels, or the middle ones, *or even the lower levels.*

Despair gripped Bell's heart as he arrived at the answer to his own question.

The cruel identity of his current location was—the thirty-seventh floor.

His trembling lips shaped a whisper.

"The deep levels..."

【LYU • LEON】
BELONGS TO: *ASTREA FAMILIA*
RACE: ELF
JOB: WAITRESS AT THE BENEVOLENT MISTRESS
DUNGEON RANGE: FORTY-FIRST FLOOR
WEAPONS: SWORD, SHORTSWORD
CURRENT FUNDS: 44,400 VALIS

STATUS

Lv. 4

STRENGTH: E488 DEFENSE: F352 DEXTERITY: A888 AGILITY: A889
MAGIC: B717 HUNTER: G IMMUNITY: G MAGIC RESISTANCE: I

《MAGIC》

【LUMINOUS WIND】
- WIDE-RANGE ATTACK MAGIC
- WIND AND LIGHT ATTRIBUTES

【NOA HEAL】
- HEALING MAGIC
- IMPACTED BY SURROUNDING ENVIRONMENT. EFFECTS ARE BOOSTED IN FORESTED AREAS.

《SKILL》

【FAIRY SERENADE】
- INCREASES IMPACT OF MAGIC
- STRONGER EFFECTS AT NIGHT

【MIND LOAD】
- DURING ATTACKS, USE OF MENTAL POWER RESULTS IN INCREASED PHYSICAL STRENGTH
- ACTIVELY TRIGGERED, INCLUDING AMOUNT OF MENTAL POWER CONSUMED

【AERO MANA】
- WHEN RUNNING, ATTACK STRENGTH INCREASES WITH SPEED
- ACTIVELY TRIGGERED, INCLUDING AMOUNT OF MENTAL STRENGTH CONSUMED

《KODACHI FUTABA》

- TWO SHORTSWORDS.
- AN EXCELLENT, EXTREMELY SHARP WEAPON EVEN AMONG SECOND-TIER GEAR.
- LYU RECEIVED IT FROM GOJONO KAGUYA, AN *ASTREA FAMILIA* MEMBER FROM THE FAR EAST. GOJONO WAS A RIVAL AND COMRADE-IN-ARMS WHO TAUGHT LYU SWORD FIGHTING.
- THE ONLY ITEM LYU CHOSE TO KEEP WITH HER IN BATTLE RATHER THAN RETURNING TO HER FAMILIA'S COMMUNAL GRAVE ON THE EIGHTEENTH FLOOR.

Afterword

I'm afraid I'm giving away all my secrets up front, but my model for the catastrophe was a certain alien queen.

The afterword to this volume is something of a confession of sins.

I offer my sincerest apologies for not managing to finish this episode in a single volume. I had planned to tell the whole story of the elven tavern waitress by the end of the book, but as usual, I found myself several hundred pages beyond the planned length, and therefore I decided to split the story into a first and second volume (plus, I thought readers might get worn out if they had to go straight through all the tight spots and bloody battles that continue after Chapter 6 without a break). I'm terribly sorry about that…

There was an omen this might happen. The main heroine this time around was supposed to be the tavern elf, but instead, the prophetess of tragedy shoved her out of the way and claimed center stage for herself. Seems she wanted to escape the shadows she had been confined to so far.

I'd thought up the "prophecies" as a sort of gimmick for the plotline early on, but once I got started, the deliverer of the prophecies just wouldn't stay still. Her despair, inner struggles, and determination went far beyond what I had initially planned, and in the end, she escaped my control for fifty pages or so. It may have been the first time words flowed so smoothly onto the page. In the end, she was promoted to quite the heroine (at least in my opinion). It was such a shock to me that I kept on mumbling to myself that it must be a mistake.

While I was bending backward to accommodate this unexpected turn of events, however, I was also a bit pleased. I suspect that it's a good thing for both the author and the book when the characters who live within the story betray the author's original plans or shoot to the forefront of their own accord. My apologies to those readers who were expecting to see more of the elven heroine, however. She'll have a larger role to play in the next volume (I think), so please hold on a little longer.

With that, I'd like to move on to acknowledgments.

To Matsumoto-sama, who is newly in charge of the series, I look forward to continuing to work with you in the future. To Editor in Chief Kitamura, I thank you for supporting me numerous times when I thought all was at an end and apologize for once again causing you so much trouble. Suzuhito Yasuda-sensei, I am deeply appreciative and impressed by the wonderful illustrations you have provided, which truly spice up the story. I especially love the illustrations of the battle rush. My thanks, as well, to everyone else involved in the production of this book. Most of all, I extend my sincerest gratitude to all the readers who decided to pick up this book.

I will do my utmost to deliver the second half of this episode as quickly as possible. I hope we meet again, and I thank you for reading this far. With that, I take my leave.

Fujino Omori